THE HUNTRESS IS DEAD

The Huntress Is Dead

A WADE PARIS MYSTERY

by Ben Benson

WILDSIDE PRESS

The Huntress Is Dead

Published by Wildside Press LLC
www.wildsidepress.com

THE HUNTRESS IS DEAD

CHAPTER

1

WHEN he came out of the gatehouse of the Norfolk Prison Colony the first thing he did was look up toward the sun. It was not that he hadn't seen the sun in his two years at the prison. Every fair day he had had the sun in the Colony quadrangle. But there was a distinction. That had been in the quad. It had not been on the outside where there were no walls, where it seemed to be a different sun, a free sun. There was no prison pallor on him, either. His suit was nondescript but it was civilian. He had money in his pocket that he had earned in the prison shops those two years. Not much, but he did have some. Perhaps the only trace of the prison was the quick shuffling step as he came down the stairs to where she was waiting. It was not the big confident stride he had once had, but more the ambling walk of a person who was accustomed to queueing up in lines, the listless step of men doing things grudgingly, against their wills.

Mrs. Wesley Cagle had been standing near the entrance

of the parking lot. When she saw him she ran to him. He stopped short.

She reached up and kissed him on the mouth. "Wes," she said simply. "You look just fine."

"I feel fine," he said to his wife. "Real fine." He took a deep breath of the early summer air. He had just lied to her. He did not feel fine at all. There were fear and depression in him. The exhilaration of freedom that he had been expecting was not there. He looked over to the high walls of the prison and he felt naked and unprotected outside of them.

"You look like a human being again," she said. She had seen him last week in the visitors' room in the Administration Building and, of course, he had not changed since. Except then he had been wearing the prison denims, and now it was his familiar brown suit and the shirt and the tie. With the suit he looked like any other person and there was no longer any need for her to be ashamed.

Wes Cagle stood there awkwardly. There was a footstep on the cement walk behind him and he turned quickly, tensely, his big hands clenching.

A man walked by them, briskly, brief case in hand. He smiled at them shortly.

"What's wrong?" she asked her husband.

He shook his head incisively. "Nothing, Ruth."

"Do you know that man?"

"No."

"Listen, Wes," she said. "You've got to remember you're on the outside now. You did your time. You don't owe any of them anything."

8

He nodded, looking down at her. She was small and compact, two years younger than he, twenty-four. Her birthday was next month and he must be sure not to forget. He looked at her soft brown hair and her big brown eyes and her nice legs. There was supposed to be a surge of desire for her. There wasn't. It didn't come. Instead that fear persisted.

They began walking. The car was angle-parked in the visitors' area. When they came to it, she said, "Do you want to drive?"

"I can't," he said. "My license expired. And before I can get another one I have to have permission from my parole officer."

"I forgot," she said. "I'll have to remember those things."

He helped her into the driver's seat and walked around to the other side. The car had been freshly washed. But it looked older and more worn and the paint had faded and the chromium was pitted with rust. Well, he thought, it was like anything else. Two years made a difference. Even the world outside looked older.

He got in beside her and slammed the door shut. "You've taken good care of the old heap," he said. "How's she running?"

His wife backed the car out slowly, carefully. "Pretty good. Al's been looking after it. He said we need new plugs and points. One tire is worn bad and we'll have to get a recap. There's a shimmy in the front wheels. Outside of that it's okay. I never drive it fast anyway."

She turned the car out on the highway that led to Route One-A. He twisted in his seat and looked back at the road and then at the high walls. There was no car following them.

"You want to eat out?" she asked him.

"Why?"

"I thought maybe you'd like to eat in a restaurant. Whatever you want, Wes."

"If you don't mind, let's go home."

"All right," she said. "I roasted a chicken just in case." She paused. "Al wants to see you."

"The hell with Al," he said dispassionately. "The hell with all your relatives."

"He's only my brother-in-law. He's married to my sister. Not a blood relation."

"I needed help two years ago," he said. "Not one of them lifted a finger. The hell with Al and all your relatives."

"All right," she said. "All right. Don't start it again."

He was silent for a moment. "You mean Al's coming over to the house?"

"Not if you don't want him."

"I don't want him."

"You keep forgetting something," she said.

"I know. His job offer is the reason I'm out on parole. His charity."

"You wouldn't have gotten out so soon otherwise. You'd still be in there."

"I'll have to thank him for his charity."

"He's a respectable businessman and he vouched for you."

"He's always acted lousy to me. Even before I went in. How do you think he'll treat me now?"

"You're too sensitive. You've got to expect those things in life."

"Because he has money and I don't? Listen, I know enough about him and his tax tricks and his business deals to have sent him up a long time ago."

"Ten minutes," she said. "You've been out of the Colony not more than ten minutes and we've started fighting all over again. Dammit, Wes, what do you expect from *me?*"

"Okay, okay," he said, subsiding. The car came onto the intersection at Route One-A and turned north toward Wrentham. Cagle looked back again. A car was coming toward them at high speed. His body became rigid. The car came abreast of them and sped by, its roof light flashing.

The car went on ahead and disappeared behind a bend. It had been a State Police cruiser in its two shades of blue. He relaxed on the seat.

"Al wants to talk to you tonight," his wife was saying.

He struggled to control his anger. Alfred Weaver, his brother-in-law. Al Weaver, short and squat, with the big cigar and the fawn-colored Stetson hat. Owner of three large car-washing places in suburban Boston. The Weaver Wash. He swallowed hard.

"All right," he said. "I'm grateful to Al for the job. What does he expect me to do? Kiss his—"

She broke in. "Being bitter isn't going to help. You used to get along with Al."

"As long as I let him ride me. And until I asked him for a loan that time."

"That's over with." Her hands tightened on the wheel.

"Now you're going to work for him. It's been hard enough as it is, without you—"

"Okay, okay," he said. "Let's not fight."

"You forget you still owe somebody money."

"Just don't worry about it," he said shortly.

"And if it wasn't for Al—"

"Sure," he said, fighting his anger. "Okay, I'm sorry."

They came into Summerton and turned left at the traffic light. The town seemed shabbier than it had been two years before. It was dirtier, sootier. At the Colony he had kept imagining it as bright and shiny, like a new coin.

When they came to the little gray, two-story house he was startled. It seemed to have shrunken and become more faded and frowsier. He looked up at the shutter on the upper left window. It was still loose and hung at an angle.

He stepped out of the car. Except for a child in a play-pen on a front lawn three houses down, the street was empty of people. He looked around carefully, warily. His wife joined him on the sidewalk.

"What's the matter?" he asked. "Where's everybody?"

"The neighbors wanted to come," she said. "But I told them to wait."

"What neighbors?"

"Mrs. McNamara, Addie Holt, Dora Ladd and the Sawyers. They'd have been here. But the first day—well, you know. They thought you'd want to get used to things first."

"Yeah, sure," he said. "Where's your sister?"

"She'll be here later."

They went up the front stairs and she unlocked the

door. Inside, the house was spotlessly clean as usual. But shabbier. He noticed the faded curtains. The worn spot on the living-room carpet was bigger.

He hung up his jacket in the hall closet and loosened his tie. She went into the kitchen. He followed her.

"Well," she said, "I'll get some dinner ready."

He went over to the cupboard and took out a glass. It was an old jelly glass. He let the water run from the tap. Not even a decent set of glasses in the house, he thought.

"There's beer in the refrigerator," his wife said.

"I'll have water," he said. She watched as he drank it. His Adam's apple moved up and down.

He wiped the edge of his mouth with the back of his hand. "Anybody call?"

"Yes, the parole officer, Mr. Tallino. He said he'll be around to see you sometime this afternoon."

"Anybody else?"

"No, nobody for you."

He thought for a moment. Then he turned and faced her. The June sun came in through the kitchen window and put blonde glints into her hair. "You look good, Ruth. I mean you've held together real nice."

"What did you expect to find?" she asked. "An old hag? I'm only twenty-three."

He grinned. "Twenty-four next month."

"As of today I'm still twenty-three. And you're twenty-six." She reached over and took his long, bony hand. "We've got a whole lifetime ahead of us, Wes."

"I don't know," he said. "I feel like about forty. It was a long time, Ruth. I couldn't live through it again."

"It's been a long time for me, too," she said. "We ought to start thinking of having a family, Wes."

"I'm thinking of that right now," he said.

The front bell rang sharply. He looked at her swiftly.

"Maybe it's the parole officer," she said.

He went through the dining room and looked out the front curtain.

"It's your brother-in-law, Al," he said, "smoking his big fat cigar. Don't answer it. He'll go away."

"He saw the car," she said. "Is my sister with him?"

"No."

"Let him in. You know how his mind works, Wes."

He went over to the front door and opened it. Al Weaver came in. His white shirt was crisp. His necktie was carefully knotted. His gray worsted suit was freshly pressed. His small, black calf shoes were well shined. The hat was a wide-brimmed, high-crowned Stetson.

They shook hands. Al Weaver didn't bother to take off his hat. He was sensitive about his rapidly thinning and receding hair.

"Why, hello, Wes," Al Weaver said. "You look good. When did you get here?"

"Just now."

"How do you feel, Wes?"

"Okay."

"It must feel good to be home," Al Weaver said. "I hope I didn't interrupt anything."

"You didn't," Wes Cagle said.

Al Weaver smiled, showing small white teeth. "Well, I can't stay long. I want you to come in to work for a couple of hours this afternoon."

"I can't," Wes Cagle said. "I've got other things to do."

"Yeah, I know you've got things to do. But I'm short on men in my Dedham place. Come on, I'll drive you over."

"I'm sorry, Al. My parole officer is coming. I'll be in tomorrow morning like I said."

"Don't stall me," Al Weaver said harshly. "I ask you to do me a favor and you give me a lot of talk. I stuck my neck out enough, giving you the job. Don't you ever forget it."

"No, you'll never let me forget it," Cagle said. "I'll be in tomorrow morning."

Ruth Cagle said to Weaver, "Honest, Al. He's expecting his parole officer."

Weaver clamped his teeth down on his cigar. For a moment he didn't say anything. Then, "You come in early tomorrow, Wes. Half-past seven."

"What if it rains?" Ruth Cagle asked. "There won't be any work."

"He's got to come in anyway."

"Will he get paid?" she asked.

"If he works he gets paid. No work, no pay. But he's got to be there."

"Al," she said quietly, "that's not the way you treat your other help."

"No," he said. "But then I don't have too many ex-cons working for me."

Wes Cagle moved toward him slowly and purposefully. His wife stepped in quickly between them. Al Weaver stood there with his small feet spread apart. She knew Al was deliberately baiting her husband, showing his power. Al had always been that way. He was the successful one in the family. Wes was the artisan, the workman, the machinist. Wes had made good pay at Wardwell Tool, but it had been a worker's pay. Now Wes had lost his seniority and Wardwell would not take him back. It would be many months before he would be in line to go to work at Wardwell again—*if* they would take him back. In the meantime, without a job Wes would not be eligible for parole. Al had pledged him a job at $1.25 an hour as a washman in one of his car laundries. No pay on rainy days. It was little enough but Wes had no choice. No job, no parole.

"Stop it, you two," she said. She had handled Al before, with the aid of her sister, Louise. Louise was tall and prim and she ruled her household firmly, including her husband.

"You listen to me, Ruth," Al was shouting angrily. "I don't have to take no crap from him. As far as I'm concerned he can go right back to Norfolk."

"Maybe I'd better belt you in the teeth and go back," Wes Cagle shouted. "I wouldn't be worse off."

"Then go the hell back," Al shouted. "Go back. I don't give a damn how Louise will carry on. I give her brother-in-law a chance and for thanks he wants to belt me in the teeth. I've had it up to here. I'm through with you. No job. Tell *that* to your parole officer."

"No," Ruth Cagle said firmly. "Now we've gone all through this before." She squeezed Al's hand hard. "Wes didn't do a thing. He lost his head for a moment. He's just out and he's all tight inside."

"He made a threatening motion."

"He's sorry. Aren't you, Wes?"

There was no sound for a moment. Then Wes Cagle said, "I'm sorry."

"All right," Al Weaver said, straightening out his jacket. "That's better. He has to understand I'm the boss. While he's working for me he's only one of the help."

"He understands," Ruth said.

"And he'd better watch that temper," Weaver said. "It'll get him in trouble."

"He'll watch it," she said. "Would you like to stay for lunch, Al?"

"No, I've got to get back."

"Why don't you and Louise come over tonight?"

"Maybe," he said. "I'll see."

He fixed his hat firmly on his head and stomped out. When the door closed Ruth Cagle turned to her husband.

"Why do you fight it?" she asked. "You know you can't win. Everything is on his side."

"Has he been coming around here?" Cagle asked.

"A couple of times. But he never—"

"Listen, I know what's on his mind. I know how he's always felt about you."

"He never touched me. Never. He was always afraid I'd tell Louise. You have to understand Al. He's not like you. He's got so little manhood that he has to show off the best he can. In front of me, in front of his help. At home he's nothing. You know."

"Never mind Al," he said. "What about Maddox? Did he call?"

"No, he didn't call. Did you expect him to?"

"He was supposed to leave a message here last night."

"He didn't call," she said.

"He will."

"He can't get blood from a stone."

"He can get blood from me."

"He wants money," she said. "Blood isn't money."

"To Dewey Maddox it is. It's bad advertising to let me get away with it. He won't let me."

"How do you know?"

"I got word at the Colony. One of the inmates."

"Then go to the police."

"The cops?" He laughed shortly. "You kidding? What would the cops do?" He lifted crossed fingers. "Dewey is like this with the cops and the politicians."

"Never you mind," she said. "We'll work out something. Now let's have some lunch."

"Might as well," Cagle said. They went back into the kitchen. As soon as they got there the telephone rang.

She looked at him.

"I'll get it," he said quickly. He went into the hallway and picked up the telephone.

She could hear his voice from where she was. But it was soft and unintelligible. She went into the hallway so that she could hear better. He saw her and turned his back. He spoke hurriedly and hung up.

"Who was that?" she asked.

"Nobody important," he said rapidly. "A guy I used to know."

"What guy?"

"You wouldn't know him." His arms hung limply, heavily, resignedly. Then his hands came up slowly, fastening his collar button and pushing his tie knot closer. "This fellow heard I was out. He might have a job for me."

"What kind of a job?" she asked.

"He didn't say. Never mind the lunch, Ruth. I'll catch something outside."

"Where are you going, Wes?"

"Out for a little while."

"Where? The parole officer is coming."

"Tell him I'll be back soon."

"Wes," she said, her voice keening. "That was Dewey Maddox, wasn't it?"

"No."

"Tell me," she insisted. "It was Maddox, wasn't it?"

"No." He picked up his jacket. "It has nothing to do with Maddox. So long, I'll be back soon."

He grabbed his hat and walked out of the house. She stood at the open door and watched him go down the front steps to the street. He went by their car and walked down to the corner bus stop. There he lit a cigarette and looked back at the house.

She closed the door and went to the dining-room window. She saw the bus come along and stop. He stepped into it. The bus started up and disappeared. Her mouth was dry and her heart was beating rapidly. She knew the call had been from Dewey Maddox. But she didn't know what she could do about it.

CHAPTER
2

Wes Cagle came into State Police Headquarters at 1010 Commonwealth in Boston. With him was the Chief of Police of Summerton, Matt Hruska.

They waited a moment at the information window. Then they were shown into the state detectives' room, where they spoke to a tall, thin, bespectacled State Police lieutenant named McKenney. From there they went with McKenney to the corridor and sat on a bench outside the Chief of Detectives' office. McKenney left them and went inside.

They waited five minutes. Then Lieutenant McKenney poked his head out of the office and motioned them to come in.

There was a man seated behind the flattop desk in the office. He had clipped sandy hair and pale-blue eyes. Wes Cagle thought him to be in his mid-thirties. The man stood up and Cagle saw he was tall and lean. He came around the desk and shook hands with Chief Matt Hruska.

"Matt," the man said, "how've you been?"

"Pretty good, Captain," Hruska said. "This is Wesley Cagle from Summerton. Wes, this is Captain Wade Paris."

Paris shook hands with Cagle, then said, "Sit down, please."

Cagle sat down. Lieutenant McKenney was standing near the window. Hruska leaned against the back wall of the office. Paris went back behind his desk and slipped into his chair. With the door closed and with everyone in civilian clothes, the police aura was gone. They were, Cagle thought, like a small group of businessmen, polite but distant and remote. He knew Hruska had already spoken to Captain Paris on the telephone.

"We're very much interested in your story," Paris said to Cagle. "Tell us a little about yourself."

Cagle looked around. Hruska had now sat down in a chair, hooking one shoe around one of the legs. McKenney was staring out onto Commonwealth Avenue.

"I'm twenty-six years old," Cagle said. "I was born and raised in Fitchburg. My father and mother died when I was young and I was raised by an uncle. He died a couple of years back. I went to Wentworth Institute in Boston and learned tool- and die-making. I did my Army service and married a Boston girl named Ruth Hoyt. That was four years ago when I was twenty-two."

"What made you decide to settle down in Summerton?" Paris asked.

"I've got no family. Ruth has a sister living there and I got a job at Wardwell's as a tool- and die-maker. So we moved there. Bought an old house."

"Any children?"

"No, sir. No kids."

"How did you get mixed up with Dewey Maddox?"

"Well, I was making pretty good money at Wardwell's but I liked to gamble. That was my big trouble. Gambling. The horses, dogs, cards, dice, the numbers, anything. It was like a sickness with me, what you'd call a compulsive gambler, I guess. Pretty soon I'd used up the few bucks we had put away and all the money I could borrow in the shop. I was only trying to get even now. Once I got even I was going to quit—"

"I know," Paris said. The man was gangly and thin, almost to the point of emaciation, Paris thought. He had a prominent Adam's apple that bobbed up and down as he talked. And he was obviously very frightened.

Cagle said, "I started to bet with Dewey Maddox and he was giving me credit. Before I knew it I was in to him for a thousand bucks and he cut me off. If he'd given me a chance to get even—"

"Go on," Paris said.

"Dewey wanted his money. I don't know if you're acquainted with him, Captain. He's a bookie around through Norwood, Westwood, Summerton. That area."

"We know of him," Paris said.

"Dewey started to call me up at the house and at the shop. He wanted his money. I told him if he kept bothering me at the shop I might get fired. He didn't care. He said the next thing he was going to do was cripple me. He could do it, too. He's big and he's an ex-heavyweight fighter. He wanted his money and he didn't care how I got it."

"Couldn't you go to friends, relatives?" Paris asked.

"I tried. No good."

22

"So you went out and pulled a stick-up," Paris said.

"Yes, sir," Cagle said. "I guess you know my record. I held up that gas station on Route One."

"Armed robbery," Paris said. "You used a gun."

"Yes, sir."

"You robbed the man of a hundred and sixty dollars," Paris said, looking down at the papers on his desk.

"Yes, sir. And I got grabbed by a state trooper as I was leaving."

"And you gave the trooper a battle."

"I got panicky," Cagle said. "I was scared what would happen to me. That trooper belted me."

"Because you hit him on the head with the gun. Didn't you?"

"I'm sorry as hell about that."

"Yes, and now you've gone to Chief Hruska about a telephone call. You want help."

"Yes, sir. I need help bad. Dewey Maddox is threatening me again." Cagle moved in his chair. "Hell, Captain, it was more than that. This time he threatened to hurt my wife, too."

"He knows you haven't got the money. How does he expect you to get it?"

"Like I said to Chief Hruska, he told me he'd give me a chance to earn it. One job for him and I'm clean."

Paris eyed him. "Why didn't you tell Chief Hruska what the job is?"

"I was scared to."

"All right, what does Maddox want you to do for him?" Paris asked.

"Murder a woman."

CHAPTER

3

WES CAGLE heard Chief Hruska's chair scrape along the floor. He turned and watched the middle-aged, short, stocky Hruska as he pulled his chair up closer to the desk. Lieutenant McKenney had turned from the window and was facing him. There was silence in the office. Outside the closed door a woman went by on her way to the commissioner's office, her heels clicking on the corridor floor.

Paris said, "He wants you to murder a woman for him?"

"Yes, sir," Cagle said.

Hruska, who had not spoken until now, asked harshly, "What woman?"

"He didn't say, Chief," Cagle said.

"Where?" Paris asked.

"He didn't tell me that either."

Hruska said, "Dammit, why didn't you tell me this before?"

"Because I was scared," Cagle said doggedly. "I wanted to get away from town before I said any more."

"All right," Paris said, "what exactly did Maddox tell you?"

"He told me I had to pay him the money I owed. I said I didn't have it and there was no way I could get it. He'd have to wait. He wouldn't wait. Then he told me he had a way I could earn it. One job. Kill a woman."

"How did he leave it?" Paris asked.

"He told me there'd be a meet."

"When?"

"Tonight at nine o'clock. That's why I took the bus to Dedham and called Chief Hruska from there. The chief met me at a diner. I wanted to make sure Maddox didn't see me."

"Where is this meet supposed to take place?" Paris asked.

"At Lake Islington."

"Exactly where at Lake Islington?"

"There's a road along the west shore just after Al's Boat Livery," Cagle said. "It's a black tar road. I'm supposed to walk down it until a car comes along and picks me up."

"Then what?" Paris asked.

"Nothing. Somebody in the car is supposed to give me orders."

"Who?"

"I don't know."

"Maddox himself?"

"He didn't say."

"How will they know you?"

"I just tell them who I am. Dewey's going to call me again at five tonight to make sure I don't chicken out."

"Why? Did you tell him you wouldn't do the job?"

"Yes, sir. I told him I didn't think I could do it."

"What did he say to that?"

"He said he'd not only cripple me, but my wife, too."

"What else?" Paris asked.

"That's all."

Paris was writing on a pad in front of him. Hruska stood up. He turned to Cagle and said, "How do you know it was Dewey Maddox talking?"

"Because I recognized his voice," Cagle said.

"You've been away in the can two years," Hruska said. "A lot of people know you owed him money. It might be a gag or something."

"I still recognized Dewey's voice."

"You wouldn't be able to swear it in court, would you?" Hruska asked.

"Yes, I could," Cagle said stubbornly.

"I mean," Hruska said, "if we picked up Maddox and he said you're crazy he never called you, it would be his word against yours, wouldn't it?"

"I guess so," Cagle said. He was beginning to feel uneasy.

"You've got no witnesses or anything," Hruska said. "Your wife didn't hear it, did she?"

"No, sir. I didn't tell her. But I know it was Dewey. I can swear it was his voice."

"And he can swear it wasn't," Hruska said.

"Why would I bring it up then?" Cagle asked. He could feel the perspiration of fear breaking out all over him. "What reason would I have?"

"You'd want to cop out on the dough you owe him,"

26

Hruska said. "You'd make the police put the heat on him."

"I wouldn't do a thing like that."

"Maddox could say you did," Hruska said. "It's his word against yours."

Cagle was silent. He looked at the emotionless face of Wade Paris and his fear grew. Dewey Maddox had not lied about his connections, he thought. He had wires right into State Police Headquarters. As high up as the Chief of Detectives.

"How many people know about this telephone call?" Paris asked him.

"Nobody but the people in this room," Cagle said. He swallowed hard, looking toward the closed door now, fearful of the hard, impassive faces. He should have lied to them and said a lot of people knew. But it was too late. If he could get away from them for a short time, he could telephone Ruth and they could meet secretly somewhere. He would have to break his parole and leave the state. Maybe in Mexico or somewhere Dewey Maddox wouldn't hunt him down. These men were in with Maddox. He could tell from their questioning. He should have listened to some of those inmates in the Colony. You never went to the police, they said. The police were your sworn enemies. Besides, what was worse, he had hit that trooper at the time of the holdup and they had been waiting to get him. He wouldn't even be surprised if Dewey Maddox himself walked in at that moment while they decided what to do with him.

"And nobody knows you came here?" Paris asked.

Cagle hesitated. He wanted to say he had told his wife

and she would worry if he didn't come home. But some-how he couldn't involve her. "No," he said.

"Good," Paris said. He looked down at his papers, then up again. "Now this is what you'll do, Cagle. You'll go right home and you'll wait for five o'clock. When Maddox calls, you tell him you can't do the job. Tell him you don't have the guts for it and you'd botch it."

"Yes, sir," Cagle said, thoroughly confused. "But—"

"Wait until I finish," Paris said. "You know somebody else who'll do the job. You'll send this other guy instead." Paris looked over at McKenney. "Who've we got?"

McKenney pursed his lips. "There's Joe Fremont."

"Too near," Paris said.

"There's Jack Barr," McKenney said. "He's fresh out of Walpole."

"That was the assault with intent to kill?" Paris asked.

"That's right, Captain," McKenney said. "Barr is out about a month. He did seven years."

"Would Maddox know him?"

"Not personally," McKenney said. "Barr is strictly a strong-arm man. The Worcester area. I'd check it first to make sure."

"All right," Paris said. "As of now it's Jack Barr." He turned to Cagle. "Jack Barr is a friend of yours. He lives in Worcester. He finished a seven-year stretch at Walpole State Prison a month ago. You know him. You tell Mad-dox you can arrange for Barr to be there instead of you."

"What if he won't go for it, Captain?" Cagle asked.

"That's the only deal," Paris said. "He has to go for it or it's nothing. Don't worry about it. He's setting up some woman as a target. He needs you more than you need him."

"If you say so—"

"We've dealt with these things before," Paris said. "Will you do as we say, Cagle?"

"Yes, sir."

"Fine. Then just go home. You do nothing and say nothing until you hear from Maddox. When he calls, you tell him what I said. You have a friend who'll do the job. If he asks the name, it's Jack Barr. B-a-r-r. From Worcester. He got out of Walpole a month ago. Only the price is up. It's twenty-five-hundred dollars. That way you take care of Barr and pay off Maddox, too. Get it? You explain it to him that way."

"Yes, sir," Cagle said. "But why?"

"There has to be a good reason for the switch. If you can get Maddox a man and square your debt, that's good thinking on your part. That's the way a man like Maddox will expect you to think. You be firm. Don't let him beat the price down. Tell him Barr will be there at the meet. Alone. You don't want to know any of the details because you want no part of the job. You understand? Don't overplay it."

"Yes, sir," Cagle said. "But what if he doesn't go for it?"

"That won't concern you," Paris said. "Either way, you're out of it. You and your wife will be protected."

"Yes, sir," Cagle said.

"All right," Paris said. "Let's go over it again—"

CHAPTER

4

WHEN he came back to Summerton he walked slowly from the bus stop to the house. Going up the creaking front stairs, he noted dispassionately that the wood of the second step was badly rotted.

The front door swept open. Ruth Cagle stood there.

"I've been sick with worry," she said. "Where did you go?"

"Into Boston," he said. He came in and put his hat on the shelf of the hall closet.

"Why didn't you tell me where?"

"I told you it was about a job. I didn't want to get your hopes up."

"You didn't get it?"

"No."

"I've been phoning Louise every ten minutes. Who was it that called you?"

"I told you before," he said. "A friend. You wouldn't know him."

"Who?"

"His name is Jack Barr. I knew him in the Army."

"You never mentioned him before."

"I hardly knew the guy. The job didn't turn out. But he's going to call me again at five. He's trying to make another connection for me."

"You should have told me before," she said. "The parole officer was here. He was good and sore you weren't home."

"What did you tell him?"

"I said you had to go see about a better job. He's coming back tonight."

"What time?"

"Eight o'clock," she said. "What about Dewey Maddox?"

He stared at her. "What about him?"

"Have you forgotten about him so soon?"

"Don't worry about him."

"That's easy to say," she said. "Did you eat?"

"In Boston," he lied.

"It's almost five now. I'll make something."

"Some ham and eggs would be fine," he said. "And some good hot coffee."

"Come in the kitchen and talk to me," she said.

He followed her. She busied herself at the stove, frying the ham. He stared at the kitchen walls. They needed painting. There was so much they did need and so little money.

"All right," she said over her shoulder. "Tell me the truth?"

"About what?"

"About where you really went. I don't believe you went

to see anybody about a job. I never heard of this Jack Barr. And besides you've got a job with Al."

"That's a hell of a job," he said. "Fifty bucks a week. Menial labor. I happen to be a top-grade machinist."

"Al got you out of the Colony."

"So I'm grateful," he burst out. "I'm grateful. I'll get down and lick his boots, that's what I'll do. What are you worrying about?"

"You know what I'm worried about," she said. "It's Dewey Maddox." She flipped the ham over in the pan and broke two eggs into it. "You're not fooling me one bit. That was Dewey who called earlier."

"You're so stubborn," he said, "I'm not going to argue with you."

She put the plate of food in front of him. He began to eat wolfishly, cramming it down. "Let's have the coffee now," he said, his mouth full.

"You didn't eat in Boston," she said, pouring the coffee for him.

"I was too busy."

"I'll go to Dewey," she said. "I'll talk to him."

"You keep away from him," he shouted, spitting flecks of food. "Stop nagging me about Dewey."

"Then I'll go to Matt Hruska."

"I'm telling you for the last time, keep out of it."

The telephone rang. He looked up at the kitchen clock. It was two minutes past five. He had trouble swallowing the food in his throat.

"I'll take it," he said, getting up quickly.

He went into the hallway and picked up the telephone. "Hello," he said.

"Is Ruth listening?" the voice asked. It was Dewey Maddox.

"No," he said.

"Where were you?"

"I had to make a connection."

"For what?"

"For the job."

"Stupid, stupid. It's *your* job."

"No, I can't handle it. I got somebody else for you."

"You're crazy," Maddox said. "You're kidding me."

"No."

"What is this? A gag?"

"No," Cagle said. "You want somebody to do the job. I've got him. But the price is up to twenty-five."

"Listen, Wes, if you're making a fool out of me—"

"It's twenty-five and somebody else. You want to listen, okay. Otherwise, I'll hang up. I don't care."

"Oh, you'll care plenty."

"I told you I don't care either way. You want to listen?"

There was a pause. Then, "What's his name?"

"Jack Barr. He's out of Walpole a month. Lives in Worcester."

"How do I see him?"

"Same way. At the meet."

"No, you arrange a talk first. I want to see you with him."

"No. I've given you this guy. He'll do it. You want him —okay. He'll meet you or whoever he's supposed to. I want no part of it. I don't even want to know what the job is. It's better for me and for you."

"Fifteen hundred."

"Twenty-five. Only one price. I've got to cop out on the dough I owe you."

"You no-good chiseling bastard. I'll fix you, Cagle."

"You mean you don't want the deal?"

"That's just what I mean."

"Okay, good-by."

"You crazy, Cagle? You know what's going to happen to you?"

"I don't care any more."

"Wait a minute, you punk. I'll call you back in fifteen, twenty minutes. I got to think about it."

The telephone clicked off. He hung up slowly. Now, for the first time, he felt the wetness of his perspiration. He walked back into the kitchen. Ruth was sitting at the table drinking a cup of coffee.

"It was getting cold," she said, "so I'm having it. I'll make you another."

"Thanks," he said. "I'll do it myself."

"Who was it?"

"Jack Barr. He has to call me back. He may have something."

"Don't keep lying to me."

"Why? Were you listening?"

"No," she said bitterly. "Why bother?"

He went over to the kitchen counter and put some instant coffee in a cup. Then he poured the hot water in and stirred absently. Dewey Maddox would now be checking up on Jack Barr.

She said, "I'd better call up Louise and tell her not to come over tonight."

"Why?"

34

"Mr. Tallino. Did you forget him? You want Louise here while the parole officer is talking to you?"

"Don't use the phone yet. I'm expecting Barr to call back."

"You don't have to be afraid of Dewey," she said. "I've been thinking it over. I'll still be working at the supermarket. Between the both of us—"

"A hundred bucks a week," he said. "Then the deductions. Then how much for food and clothes and the car and light and heat and telephone and the mortgage on the house? How much are you going to pay off?"

"Twenty dollars a week. I've been figuring it out. I don't need any clothes. We don't need the car. Twenty dollars a week I'll give him. In two years we've got him paid off. I'll go myself and tell him."

"You're nuts if you think he'll listen to you."

"He will."

"Sure. He left word at the Colony that he wants all the money by the end of this week. And how about your dental work? The molars you had out? You need some bridgework. How much is that going to cost? And where are you going to get the money? From your brother-in-law, Al?"

"Maybe if I speak to Louise once more."

"And maybe I'll start digging in the back yard so we can strike oil. Wake up. When you're talking to Louise and Al you're talking to two stones."

He drank his coffee. He had forgotten to add sugar. But his taste for it was gone anyway. He said, "You stop worrying about Dewey Maddox. To tell the truth, I spoke to Matt Hruska."

"Yes?" she asked, her cup poised. "When?"

35

"Before I went into Boston. Honest. He said he'd watch out. He'd talk to Dewey."

"You shouldn't have done it," she said. "Matt will only steam up Dewey against you. Dewey will give Matt Hruska a big smile and say, 'Aw, Wes don't owe me a cent, Matt. Somebody's kidding you. Wes is my pal.' Then some night somebody's waiting for you with a piece of lead pipe. It won't be Dewey. He'll be with a girl in a bar that night. Don't you think I know?"

The telephone rang again. He went into the hallway and picked up the phone. "Hello?"

"Don't mention no names," Dewey Maddox's voice said. "Your friend know where to meet?"

"I told him."

"How come he's not home?"

"What did you do? Call him?"

"I got friends in Worcester."

"You didn't have to call him."

"I don't trust you. Why ain't he home?"

"Because I told him to come on in. If there was no deal I'd pay his bus fare back."

"What's the matter? Don't this big operator even have a car?"

"He's just out. They won't let him. If he needs a car he'll snatch one. That's between you and him. Not me."

"I don't like it, you bastard."

"Don't meet him then. Forget it."

"It's worth two grand. That's a lot. Double what you were going to get."

"He has to get fifteen," Cagle said. "He won't do it for less. And he collects twenty-five. He passes my share over to me and I pay it back to you. That way there's no mistake and we both know the deal."

"Twenty-three hundred," Maddox said.

"Twenty-five," Cagle said. "Or forget it."

"You cheap punk," Maddox said. "Cheap, lousy punk. He don't get the money until the job's done."

"I already told him."

"How come you know so much, you cheap punk?"

"I know *you*."

"Tell him to be there," Maddox said. He hung up.

Wes Cagle cradled the telephone slowly. He was realizing for the first time that he had been afraid these past several years for nothing. Dewey Maddox was a frightened, nervous man, a big, blustering hulk with a bad mouth. He was, Wes Cagle thought, nothing but a small-time hoodlum who had put up a big bluff.

He went into the kitchen and he now felt hungry again. He looked at his wife standing near the sink. He went over, lifted her and swung her around.

"Honey," he said, laughing, "everything is going to be all right."

Then, as he put her down, he wondered for the first time who the woman was that Dewey Maddox wanted murdered.

CHAPTER

5

Trooper Frank Montaigne stood in the office of the commander of C Troop. The headquarters of C Troop, Massachusetts State Police, was in the town of Holden outside the city of Worcester. The commander of the troop was Captain Eboli. He sat behind his desk and looked at Montaigne carefully.

Montaigne was standing with his highly polished, black field boots apart, his hands clasped behind his back in a position of parade rest. His dark-blue whipcord breeches were taut and freshly pressed. His pale-blue blouse was immaculate and the silver buttons on it gleamed. His dark-blue campaign hat was set squarely on his head. He was a dark, wiry young man of twenty-seven, five feet, ten inches tall, and he weighed a hundred and sixty pounds. His eyes were dark, his face was intense and his mouth a thin, hard slash.

"That's the story," Captain Eboli said to him. "Any questions, Montaigne?"

"No, sir," Montaigne said, in a flat, toneless voice.

"Then that's all," Captain Eboli said. "Good luck."

"Yes, sir," Montaigne said. He brought his heels together, turned and went out.

Eboli looked thoughtfully at the empty doorway. Montaigne never had questions, he thought. You gave him a job and he did it. If you didn't give him a job, he would ask for one. Any job of investigation, the most tedious, the most difficult, the most hazardous, Montaigne wanted it. He was a man who drove himself constantly, barely civil and articulate with his fellow troopers. No camaraderie, no horseplay. He avoided personal contact. He roomed by himself and, when he could, he did most of his patrols alone. If he stopped a motorist for a traffic violation or a routine check, anything the motorist said was to a deaf ear. He was not discourteous. There never was a complaint of that. He just did not see the motorist as a human being but as a part of the vehicle he drove. He was troubled with insomnia and had an utter disdain of personal safety. Once a woman, overweight and middle-aged, had fallen out of a boat on a lake. Montaigne had come up in his cruiser and, not waiting to remove the spare tire and use it as a life preserver, had dived in. His boots had become heavy and waterlogged but he had brought in the half-drowned woman, fighting fiercely for her life when he had such disregard for his own. There was the time of a prison mutiny in one of the shops at Walpole. When the order was given to the troopers to go in, Montaigne had been the first to smash the window glass with his rifle butt and vault over the four-foot-high, brick, side wall of the shop, bulling inside and tackling the mutiny leader. And there was the time when in a cruiser alone he had stopped three

39

known armed holdup men. He had gone for them without taking any cover. Later, one of the prisoners said he had been terrified by the expression on Montaigne's face.

The rashness, Eboli thought, meant only one thing. It was as though Montaigne was seeking death deliberately. And the way he was going, Eboli knew it would not be long before he found it. But if they wanted a man to take the place of Jack Barr, there was none better. The change in Montaigne had started when he had lost his wife in an automobile accident over a year ago. From then on he had become morose, silent, indrawn, doing his job well but with no vestige of any human touch. It could not keep up, Captain Eboli thought. He had tried to talk to Montaigne and had failed to reach him. Somebody should. Somebody should before it was too late. He did not want to lose one of his best men.

Frank Montaigne was in his room on the floor above the captain's office. The bed was neatly made, garrison style. On the dresser was a set of silver-backed military brushes with his initials on them. They had been a gift from his wife, Doris. Other than those and the curtains on the windows, the room was free of any ornamentation. It was sparse and bare, like a monk's cell.

He sat down on the stiff-backed chair and buried his face in his hands for a moment. Then he stood up and started to undress, taking out the bootjack from the dresser drawer and pulling off his boots. He kept thinking back to Doris, of the argument and how stupid it had been, and how arrogant and intolerant he had acted.

But there was no going back—ever. No way of living it over, no starting off again.

He had met Doris in England when he had been stationed in her town. It was a missile site. The Army duty had been routine and he had been able to spend quite a bit of time with her. They had been married in an Anglican church. When his tour of duty was up, Patricia had been born. He returned to the States with his wife and daughter and he had passed the examinations successfully and had enlisted in the State Police.

At the time of the incident they had been living in Natick and he had been assigned to A Troop. That evening he had come home after three days in a swamp, with a posse and bloodhounds, searching for a lost child. The child had been found in a shallow pool of brackish water, whimpering, hungry, insect-bitten, but alive. And when he had arrived at his house, his own daughter, Patty, was not at home.

He had been very tired and irritable and he had just come from a case of negligence and carelessness on a mother's part. He asked where Patty was. Doris said she was staying at a friend's house. He was very angry. He had had no sleep for two days and was dirty and unshaven. And the family where Patty was staying was lackadaisical and slovenly, like that of the family whose child he had just found.

He demanded that Doris go over and fetch Patty immediately. Doris objected. The child was playing with her little friend and had planned to sleep over there because she had not known when her father would be home. Doris said it was a little holiday for the child. Montaigne demanded that she go get Patty. There were words. Then there were louder and angrier words and Montaigne, half-numb with fatigue, for the first time, slapped his wife and ordered her to get the child.

Doris looked at him with shocked eyes, then grabbed her coat and fled the house to pick up Patty. In her shock and hurt, she automatically must have reverted to the British way of driving. Because she raced down the left side of the road instead of the right, crashed head-on into a trailer truck and was instantly killed.

He was never the same after that. Because his mother lived in Auburn in the C Troop area, he moved out of Natick and asked for a transfer. They assigned him to Holden. He would never talk to anybody about what had happened, turning away from any words of solace or attempts to help him. He tried to act as both father and mother to Patty, but he was inadequate for it. His mother brought the child up.

He had removed his uniform now and he put on his civilian sports shirt, slacks, shoes and jacket. Then he examined himself in the mirror. Somehow the clothes were too clean and the shoes too burnished. He would go down to the rear of the barracks, scuff up the shoes, wrinkle the shirt and rub the slacks with dust.

He hung up his uniform in the closet, checked his revolver and put it back on the shelf, then locked the closet door. He looked slowly around the room. Everything was in its proper place. He went out and down the stairs.

CHAPTER
6

It was evening now. Ruth Cagle watched the street from the dining-room window. Every so often she had seen a sand-colored sedan pass the house. There was a man in the car whom she could not recognize. It worried her. It would be just like Dewey Maddox to have someone keep an eye on the house, waiting for the right opportunity.

As it grew darker she could no longer stand in the dining room and watch an occasional car swish by. She went into the hallway. From the living room she could hear the voices of Wes and the parole officer, Mr. Tallino. Tallino was a mild, serious, bespectacled young man from the Department of Correction. She listened to them talking for a moment. Mr. Tallino was giving Wes certain rules of conduct that he must follow.

She went to the telephone and dialed her sister's number. "Louise," she said softly. "Where's Al?"

"Al?" her sister asked. "He's at the car-wash place in Westwood. Why?"

"I have to talk to him."

"If it's the same old business—"

"Louise, you don't realize it. Dewey Maddox is still after Wes. He wants his money."

"I told you not to talk about it any more," Louise Weaver said angrily. "I'm sick of it. You hear? Sick of it."

"We appreciate everything you and Al have done for us. But we need the money, Louise."

"Al can't spare it. We've told you time and time again, his money's tied up in the business."

"Maybe if he just spoke to Dewey. He knows Dewey."

"No," Louise Weaver said. "You keep Al out of this. I don't want him to have anything to do with Dewey Maddox."

"How would it be if you called Dewey, Louise?"

"Me? Why me?"

"You went out with him once."

"That was a long time ago," Louise shouted. "You have no right to bring it up. That's acting pretty low if you ask me."

"I'm sorry, but I'm desperate, Louise."

"That was an insulting thing to say to me," Louise Weaver said. "I wouldn't have the stomach to even talk to someone like Dewey Maddox. And if I did, it would do no good."

"What am I going to do, Louise?"

"Why don't *you* talk to him? Dewey always had an eye for you—"

"You're not serious, Louise."

"Yes, I am," Louise Weaver said. "I have to say good-by now. The baby is cranky. I'll call you tomorrow."

Louise Weaver hung up. Ruth Cagle put down the

44

phone slowly. She went out of the hallway and back to the darkened dining room. Looking out the window she thought she saw a strange car parked at the corner of the street near the bus stop.

She went swiftly into the bathroom and put on lipstick. She knew what she had to do.

Trooper Frank Montaigne stood in front of Captain Wade Paris in his office at State Police Headquarters. The costume was appropriate, Paris thought. Montaigne was wearing a soiled sports jacket, wrinkled pants, a sports shirt and a pair of scuffed shoes. He appeared nondescript.

Paris walked around him slowly. The trooper was as tall as Barr and weighed approximately the same. He would carry no weapon of any kind and no identification.

"You understand what you have to do," Paris said, going back to his desk and sitting on the edge of it. "You've got to try to get the name and address of the woman who's to be killed and the people who want to kill her. Do the best you can without pressing it too hard. This might be only a preliminary meet."

"Yes, sir," Montaigne said.

Paris glanced at him. The boy seemed fey, as though there were an air of death around him. The face was tense, the mouth rigid. For a moment Paris had misgivings about him. But he knew the trooper was a man who did his job well. The personal tragedy in his life was unfortunate but it would not impair Montaigne's efficiency.

"Turn around," Paris said. "Move your shoulders and arms, please."

Montaigne turned slowly, flexing his shoulders and

45

swinging his arms. In the inside breast pocket of his jacket he was carrying a battery-powered, transistor radio transmitter. The transmitter was very small and was concealed in a five-pack of cigars. There were two cigars in the carton. The antenna from it went up inside the shoulder of the jacket and down the left sleeve.

"Good," Paris said. "Nothing shows. Do you smoke cigars?"

"No, sir."

"That's all right. You can be chewing on a cigar stub. It doesn't have to be lit."

"Yes, sir," Montaigne said. "A cigar stub."

"Now if somebody searches you and finds the cigar pack, offer him a cigar. Just slide the cigar out and give it to him. If he grabs the pack and pulls it out of the pocket, the antenna will disconnect. There'll be nothing to make him suspicious. The transmitter is very lightweight. You understand?"

"Yes, sir," Montaigne said. "I'll do as you say, Captain."

"Fine," Paris said. "Now you go talk to Lieutenant McKenney. And, good luck."

Montaigne left the office. Paris sat down behind his desk and looked at his check list. Jack Barr had already been picked up by two state detectives out of the Worcester office. He would be in their custody until half-past nine, and, by now, should have had a good dinner. Barr's landlady had been instructed to say, if anyone called, that Jack Barr had gone into Boston.

The remainder was up to his men, mostly to Trooper Frank Montaigne. He was the one who would be in direct contact, armed only with his bare hands.

46

CHAPTER

7

TROOPER FRANK MONTAIGNE got off the bus as it came by Lake Islington on its way to Summerton. There were a half-dozen passengers on the bus but none paid heed to him.

He walked down the road that led to the lake. The area was almost deserted. The air was cool. The sky was cloudy, obscuring a moon that had appeared earlier. The weather report had called for scattered showers.

Montaigne came to the lake. There was a row of street lights leading to a deserted, public parking area. A cold breeze off the lake fluffed at his face. The water was choppy. He put his hands in his pockets and walked up past the parking area to Al's Boat Livery. He looked at the large boathouse that rested on pilings. A float slanted down to the water. He walked by, passing a group of cottages. They were dark. There was a beach stand that was boarded up.

He walked on. A narrow, black macadam road veered to the left. There were no street lights here. He walked, his footsteps echoing on the hard pavement. Through an occasional patch between the pines, he could see the darker surface of the lake. He passed one cabin after another. Some were freshly painted, the lawns cut, ready for summer occupancy. Others were still boarded up. All of them were dark.

The road turned slightly to the right and he could no longer see the lake. The growth of trees was thicker. Now he came to another clearing. Here there were a group of cottages and a row of stores. There was a network of little dirt lanes running in every direction. He knew now why Maddox had picked this area. It was a spot that made roadblocks almost impossible.

The buildings were unlighted. He slowed his walk, listening. From behind him in the distance he heard the whine of a car. The sound came nearer. He could see the reflection of the headlights dancing on the tops of the trees. The car came closer. He stopped along the side of the road. The headlights hit him, blinding him. He turned away and waited. The car stopped with shrieking brakes a little ahead of him.

He went toward it. It was a green Chrysler sedan. He read the license number on the back plate. Dewey Maddox's car.

The door on the driver's side opened and somebody got out. The door slammed. Somebody came toward him. Montaigne looked at the man. He was standing near the rear of the car, the number-plate lights giving some reflection to his features. He was big, with heavily muscled shoulders and large hands. The bridge of the nose had been broken and flattened some time ago. There was scar tissue above the eyes. But Montaigne could see that he had the strong masculinity that would attract women.

The man said, "Who are you?"

"Jack Barr," Montaigne said belligerently, shifting the cigar butt between his teeth. "Who the hell are you?"

"Dewey Maddox," the man said.

The cold wind blew around Montaigne, rustling the new leaves on the trees. He put his hands deep into his jacket pockets.

"Come over near the light," Maddox said.

"You come over here," Montaigne said. "I'm nobody's servant."

"I've got to see what you look like," Maddox said.

Montaigne moved closer. He said, "I don't go for all this cloak-and-dagger crap out here in the middle of nowhere. Tell me what you want and let's get the hell out of here."

"My client likes to be careful," Maddox said. "Very careful. Anybody follow you?"

"Yeah, you did. I didn't see anybody else."

"I watched you get off the bus."

"I didn't see you," Montaigne said.

"I was parked behind a big garage."

"Nice," Montaigne said. "You made me walk all this way for nothing."

"Not for nothing," Maddox said. "My client wants to be careful. What price did Wes tell you?"

"Twenty-five hundred."

"The price is two grand."

"My end is fifteen hundred," Montaigne said, moving the dead cigar butt in his mouth. "And I collect a grand

49

for Wes. That's the deal. Don't cut the price now, Maddox."

Maddox was silent for a moment. Then he said, "Put your arms up."

"Why?" Montaigne asked.

"I've got to make sure you're all right." He patted Montaigne, running his hands down the sides and legs. "Ain't you carrying anything?"

"What for?" Montaigne asked. "I ain't afraid of you. Besides, I'm just out of Walpole. I'd look stupid if some cop stopped me and gave me a quick frisk."

"What's this?" Maddox asked, feeling the breast pocket.

"Cigars," Montaigne said tightly. "What's the matter? There's a law against smoking or something?"

"Got to be careful," Maddox said.

"You're pretty nervous for a guy who's supposed to have been around."

"I'll tell you the truth," Maddox said. "I don't go for this kind of jazz myself. But my client set up the play. How do you know Wes Cagle?"

"I know him through friends. That's enough of that. You want to talk business, talk business—"

"I wanted to make sure," Maddox said.

"Who's your client and who does he want hit—" Montaigne heard a twig snap and looked up. He saw a middle-sized figure standing by the car. The figure was weirdly dressed. Over the face and head was a tight-fitting black nylon stocking that distorted the nose, mouth and ears beyond recognition and made identification impossible. On top of the head was a black felt hat. The remainder of the costume was a black crewneck sweater, black pants and an oversized black jacket.

"Who's the creep?" Montaigne asked.

"My client," Maddox said.

"Why the hell's he wearing that crazy get-up for?"

"My client likes to be careful," Maddox said.

CHAPTER

8

At 8:40 that night, Lieutenant Philip Norton, supervisor of the State Police Ballistics Bureau, was sitting in an unmarked cruiser with Chief Matt Hruska of Summerton. Hruska had just finished talking with Detective Lieutenant Joe McKenney on the short-wave radio. Now he turned and watched Norton adjust the battery-powered, pack radio receiving unit.

The unit was in a leather case the size of a thin book. It had been set on the established frequency of the transmitter Montaigne was carrying, its wire attached to the cruiser's antenna. The range was about one mile.

They were behind a big cottage just off Lake Avenue, which ran along the east shore of Lake Islington. The location was a quarter of a mile away from the public parking area and Al's Boat Livery.

Norton put on the earphones. He adjusted a small, portable, battery-powered tape recorder which was about the size of an 8-mm. movie camera.

Hruska said, "You receiving him?"

"Not yet," Norton said. "We've got time. He's not in range." He turned off the tape recorder. "Who's Al Weaver?"

"Cagle's brother-in-law," Hruska said. "He gave Cagle the job so he could make parole."

"Nice guy?"

"No," Hruska said. "A sharpshooter. I was telling Paris that Weaver is in hock on those car-wash places. Dewey Maddox is supposed to be holding a mortgage on them."

"All one happy family," Lieutenant Norton said. "Anything else?"

"Yeah," Hruska said. "I think Weaver goes for Ruth Cagle. Is it all right to talk while you've got on those phones?"

"Sure," Norton said. "How come Maddox is pressing Cagle so hard?"

"Well," Hruska said, rubbing his jaw slowly, "it reminds me of the guy who owns the package liquor store down near the Wardwell factory. Wardwell has some part-time porters and sweepers who are winos. They come into the store for a pint of muscatel or port. Now a pint of wine is forty-five cents. Those winos will come in and wipe their noses and shuffle around. Then they'll start emptying their pockets. Out comes stubs of pencils, pieces of string, cigarette butts, movie stubs, and finally the coins. They'll move the coins around on top of the counter like they're playing checkers, trying to make it come out to forty-five cents. Lots of times they'll have only forty-two or -three cents, or even forty-four. They'll look at the owner and tell him they're a little short today. They'll bring in the balance the next day. After all, they tell him, look at all the liquor he's got. He's rich. He won't miss a couple of pennies. But the owner always pushes the coins back. He's learned his lesson the hard way. Once he lets them clip him, he's a goner. Word gets around that he's a soft touch. Soon they're handing him thirty-nine cents, then thirty-seven, then they're putting it on the cuff. He has to be firm. The winos know they have to have the exact amount or no bottle. I figure it's the same with Dewey Maddox. Wes Cagle is into him for a thousand bucks. If Wes Cagle beats him for it, word gets around. The next guy wants a break and so on. Soon Dewey Maddox is out a lot of dough."

"Maddox give you much trouble?" Norton asked.

"No," Hruska said. "We grabbed him once or twice when he first started to book numbers. And he's got a kid working for him, a crippled boy named Ducky Britt. Ducky's a little weak in the head and we've picked him up, too. But lately we haven't been able to do a thing. Maddox now has a little real-estate office upstairs over the bank, the Summerton Savings and Loan Association. Two rooms, an inside office and an outside office. All right, I'm a cop. I know what goes on in my town. Maddox used to box a little. He didn't have it so he went to work in Wardwell's. After a while he began to book numbers there. We picked him up, he was fined and Wardwell let him go. He went into the real-estate business as a front. He's still booking bets on the number pool and the horses. His wife divorced him five years ago and moved away. They had no kids."

"Any girl friends?"

"One or two. From around Boston. None from Summerton. The town's too small."

54

"What about his ex-wife?"

"She lives in California. I think he owes her alimony but she doesn't press it. He's living alone in a flat on Avalon Street. He owns the apartment building. During the day he's at his real-estate office over the bank. That's where he transacts his business, his loans, everything. People go in and out all the time."

"Tough to make a pinch?" Norton asked.

"Yeah," Hruska said. "I grab him once in a while. But it's real tough. This is a small town and it's growing. But the police department doesn't. I've still got the same five men. There's a lot of work to do and I don't have the manpower for it. Besides, I never get a complaint against Maddox. Sure, I hear rumors. People tell me all kinds of stories. My men report on his activities, but there's no evidence. From time to time I've put a plant on his office. We've gone in there."

"What did you find?" Norton asked.

"Sure, he's got a list of names, and numbers beside them. We know it's some kind of code, but we can't prove it. He tells us that those are real-estate prospects and the numbers are his own private rating of them. I've had the office watched. The hell of it is they go in by the bank and upstairs. Upstairs there are other offices, too."

"What about the owner of the building?"

"Maddox owns that building, too." Hruska grinned suddenly. "Today we got our first break."

He was speaking of the tap on Wesley Cagle's telephone. Cagle had given them permission and they had cut into the line early, before five. When the call had come through they had listened and recorded it.

"And that was Dewey Maddox's voice," Norton said. "No mistake?"

Hruska grinned again. "No mistake. That was Dewey. He was careful not to say anything, though. He kept talking about a 'deal' and a 'job.' He wouldn't stick his neck out—"

Norton held up his hand, cutting Hruska off. He pressed his other hand against the earphones. "I've got a faint signal," Norton said. "Montaigne is coming into range. He just said something to the bus driver."

They waited silently. Norton said, "He's walking. I can hear his footsteps now."

Hruska picked up the short-wave telephone and depressed the button. "Happy to Mulberry."

"Mulberry," the answer came back.

"He's on his way," Hruska said. "Off."

Mulberry was Lieutenant Joseph McKenney, who was in a black, unmarked cruiser with Detective-Lieutenant Walter Franz. They were parked off the road in a wooded area, not far from Al's Boat Livery. They had a good view of the public parking lot.

Norton listened on the earphones intently. Beside him the tiny tape-recorder spools rotated slowly. "He's still walking."

The short-wave radio rasped and Lieutenant McKenney's voice came on. "He just came by us."

Hruska waited. McKenney was running the show and he was the focal point.

"He's still walking," Norton said.

Hruska pushed the short-wave phone button and repeated, "He's still walking."

56

The speaker rasped back instantly. McKenney's voice said, "A car started up. It was parked behind the parking lot. It's coming by us . . . A green Chrysler. Couldn't catch the number."

"Was it an Imperial?" Hruska asked.

"Imperial," McKenney said.

"Dewey Maddox's car," Hruska said. "License number is 0718."

Norton held up his hand. "I can hear the car," he said. "It's stopped. Sounded like a door slamming—"

Norton kept speaking, reporting the conversation between Montaigne and Dewey Maddox. Hruska repeated it into the short-wave telephone to Lieutenant McKenney. McKenney listened, his face grim and taut. When he heard about the third party at the scene and the description of the costume, he looked worriedly at Lieutenant Franz, who sat behind the wheel of the cruiser.

Lieutenant Franz started the cruiser and kept the motor running. There was little else they could do at the moment.

CHAPTER

9

MONTAIGNE faced the two of them, Maddox big and hulking, the other figure smaller and grotesque.

Montaigne said, "What's the matter with your crazy friend? Don't he talk?"

"Leave my client out of it," Maddox said. "You do business with me."

"Okay," Montaigne said. "Tell me the job and when I get paid."

"You get paid after it's done."

"I've got to have sweetening money first," Montaigne said.

"Why?"

"I've got expenses."

"A hundred bucks now. The rest when the job's done."

"Five hundred now."

"Don't be a hog, Barr. You know where hogs end up."

"You scare me," Montaigne said. "All right, two-fifty on account."

"Hogs end up hung on a hook," Maddox said.

"Two hundred now," Montaigne said. "Go ahead, ask your client if it's okay. What's the matter? Ain't he got a tongue?"

"Knock it off," Maddox said. "All right, two hundred now."

"Okay, let's see the color of your money, Maddox."

"When we get through talking."

"I'm through talking now," Montaigne said. "Who's the broad you want knocked off?"

"What are you going to use?" Maddox asked.

"That's *my* business," Montaigne said. "Come on, come on, who's the broad?"

"A woman at the Summerton Hospital," Maddox said.

"All right, give me her name," Montaigne said. "Let's get it over with—"

The person in black moved. Montaigne saw a gun come out, rising, pointing. He flung himself forward at it. Too late. The gun flashed, blinding him, searing, the bullet striking his head. He started to go down, his legs would not obey him. The gun exploded again. He was hit with a terrible burning force in the chest. It felt like a jack hammer. He went to his knees. A sickness went through him. The pain was bad, enveloping him. He was going to die, he thought, and his daughter, Patty, would be alone. Patty. Little Patty . . .

Lieutenant Norton heard the shot on the earphones. "Shooting," he said to Hruska.

The short-wave radio spoke instantly. "I heard shots," McKenney said. "We're going in. Come on. If you see the Imperial, stop it."

"Coming in," Hruska said.

Norton had taken off the earphones and had started the car. The lights went on and the car slowed up onto the road, racing as best it could along the narrow winding surface.

"We'll come in behind them," Hruska said.

Norton accelerated the rocketing car. If he saw a car coming toward them he would veer into it and force it off the road. There was no car coming. The twisting road ahead was empty. But there were many dirt trails leading off it.

He kept to the hard-surfaced road as it swung around the lake. The direction he was taking would bring him into McKenney's approaching car, pinching off both ends of the paved road.

As he swung around a bend, he saw headlights ahead. The headlights were motionless. He slowed, tires squealing. The car was parked in the middle of the road. A shadow flitted by in front of it.

He jammed the car to a stop and was out of it, revolver in hand. With him came Chief Hruska with his gun out.

Flat on his back in the middle of the road was Trooper Frank Montaigne. He was bleeding from the head. His jacket was open and blood was seeping through his shirt in a widening blotch. On his knees in front of him was Detective-Lieutenant McKenney.

Norton came up quickly. "Where's he hit?" he asked McKenney.

"In the head and chest." McKenney was making a compress with his handkerchief. "Walt's radioing for an ambulance cruiser."

"How bad is he?" Norton asked.

"Very bad," McKenney said. "I won't move him without an ambulance cruiser."

"Conscious?" Norton asked.

"No," McKenney said. "He was out when we got here. You didn't see the other car?"

"No," Norton said. He looked at Hruska.

"Dammit," Hruska said, "there's a dozen little dirt roads out of here. We'll have to look for tire tracks."

Lieutenant Walter Franz came back. "There's a patrol cruiser on the way," he said. He looked down at the unconscious Frank Montaigne.

"Let's move," Lieutenant McKenney said tersely. "Matt, where's the nearest hospital?"

"Summerton," Hruska said.

"I'll send Walt there," McKenney said. He turned to Norton. "You, Phil, get over to Maddox's house and bird dog it." He swung around to Walter Franz. "Did you send out a GA on Maddox's car?"

"Yes," Franz said. "And roadblocks."

"How many?" Hruska asked. "There are five roads into Summerton from here."

"The hell I don't know it," McKenney said, without bitterness. The roadblocks would probably be ineffective. They had botched the job all the way and a trooper now lay dying.

CHAPTER
10

THE AMBULANCE patrol cruiser came in from the Foxboro Barracks. Montaigne was given first aid by the two uniformed troopers. He was then put carefully onto the folding stretcher and covered with a blue blanket. They slid him into the cruiser and rushed him to the Summerton Hospital. When he arrived there he was still unconscious. The two troopers stayed with him to guard him.

A cruiser from the Framingham Barracks arrived at Lake Islington, and the men started to search the vicinity of the shooting. Shortly afterward a station wagon came from the Framingham Barracks with a portable searchlight on a trailer. The marshaling of the state and local police forces began.

Detective-Lieutenant Joe McKenney drove his car downtown into Summerton. It had started to drizzle and a fine mist haloed the street lamps and dampened the pavement. On North Main Street was the fifty-year-old, red-brick building that housed the Summerton Savings and Loan Association. The big plate-glass window on the first floor showed a night light. He looked up to the second floor. Four of the long narrow windows were lighted.

He pulled up to the curb and stopped. In front of him was a green Chrysler Imperial sedan with its lights out. The license plate read 0718.

McKenney stepped quickly out of the cruiser and walked over to the Imperial. He opened the front door. A dome light went on. The car was empty. There were no keys in the ignition. He closed the door and moved along to the front. He felt the hood. It was warm.

He stood for a moment looking up at the lighted windows of the building. Suddenly the downstairs door opened. A woman came out. She wore a tan poplin raincoat and a plastic rain hood over her head. She hurried across the street to where an old gray Chevrolet was parked. She got into the car, started it, put on the lights and drove off. McKenney caught the license number as it went by: 097137. He jotted it down in his notebook.

He crossed the sidewalk to the entrance of the building. Inside, he saw a pair of glass doors on the right. They carried gold lettering that said *Summerton Savings and Loan Association*. Through the doors he saw the light burning over the wall safe; the shiny, waxed, asphalt-tile floor; the dark-wood, chest-high counters; the long tables with pens on them at the end of chains. To his left in the foyer there was an information board on the wall: *County Finance, Quick Loans, 1. R.A. Annis, D.D.S., 2. Elmora Dean, Attorney, 3. Dewey Maddox, Real Estate, 4. Bera's Beauty*

Bar, 5. Proctor McHugh, Photography, 6. There was a long, steep flight of wooden stairs ahead of him.

He started up. When he reached the top he saw a dimly lighted corridor. The dark-wood floor had been recently oiled.

He went by the frosted-glass doors. *County Finance, Quick Loans* was dark. So were *Elmora Dean, Attorney, Bera's Beauty Bar* and *Proctor McHugh, Photography.* But the office of *R. A. Annis, D.D.S., walk in* was lighted. He could hear the slight humming sound of a dental burr. He went by.

He unbuttoned his jacket and loosened the Chief's special revolver in its stiff, black leather, hip holster. He took out the gun and pushed the door open wider. He stood to the side of it and surveyed the room. There were a long wooden bench, six wooden chairs, a dusty window, a table with an artificial plant on it and a few dog-eared magazines.

Beyond was a thick oak door. The door was open and led to another lighted room. McKenney stepped into the office. He could hear the buzzing sound of the dentist's drill, two doors away. He walked across the office and looked into the other room quickly.

Lying on the floor of the inner office was a man. He was on his back, his eyes wide open and staring. Under the man was an ever-spreading mass of blood that was being absorbed into the cheap beige, cotton rug. The man's jacket was open, showing a white shirt with a blackened hole in the middle, the fabric cross-torn and burned. A small pattern of blood had formed around the wound.

McKenney bent and felt the pulse. There was none, but the skin had a slight warmth. He looked at the man, at the massiveness of the shoulders, the broken nose and the scar tissue above the eyes. It was Dewey Maddox and he was dead.

CHAPTER

11

It was one o'clock in the morning. Captain Wade Paris entered the gray-brick apartment building at 101 Avalon Street in Summerton. In the foyer he looked at the names on the mailboxes. Dewey Maddox was Apartment 21.

He walked up to the second floor. The door to Apartment 21 was open. He went in.

A technical sergeant from State Police Headquarters named Blackburn was taking flashbulb pictures with a camera. He turned and looked at Paris.

"How are you and Harry doing?" Paris asked.

"Pretty near through, Captain," Blackburn said.

"This the way you found the place?" Paris asked.

"Yes, sir."

Paris' eyes swept the living room. The pillows of the sofa and chairs had been tossed to the floor. A breakfront cabinet stood against one wall. The drawers were open and silverware was scattered on the gray broadloom carpeting in front of it.

Paris walked into the bedroom. The lights were on.

There, too, the drawers of the chest were open. Clothing was scattered over the floor. In the corner was a small desk. Papers were strewn all around.

He went into the kitchen. Another technical sergeant named Harry Kazanjian was there. He was standing at the formica-topped counter brushing drinking glasses for fingerprints.

"How's it going, Harry?" Paris asked.

"A lot of prints all over the place," Kazanjian said. "Somebody was sure looking for something."

There was a small, metal file box on the counter. Its little lock had been forced and broken.

"It was busted open, Captain," said Kazanjian. "That's the way we found it."

"Have you dusted it yet?"

"Yes. It's clean."

Paris picked it up. Inside was a sheaf of papers held together with an elastic band. In the bottom of the file box were two keys that seemed to be from safety-deposit boxes. Paris started through the sheaf of papers. On top was a life-insurance policy that had expired. The beneficiary had been a Mrs. Alma Maddox. There was an honorable discharge from the Navy and two savings-account books. One was on a bank in Westwood, totaling six thousand dollars. The other was on the Summerton Savings and Loan Association for two thousand dollars. There was a checking account book on the Norfolk County Trust Company that showed a balance of $735.43. There was an insurance policy on the apartment with a personal-property floater. The other papers were of no significant importance.

"Have you checked these papers yet?" Paris asked.

"Not yet," Kazanjian said.

"There's an insurance policy here with an inventory of Maddox's belongings," Paris said.

"I'll check against it to see what's missing."

"Good. And there are two safety-deposit keys."

"I'll tag them for you, Captain."

"Fine," Paris said. "I'll be over at the Summerton Police Department."

At 2 A.M. Paris was sitting in the office of the Chief of Police of Summerton. The police station was new, a small building of red brick, two stories high with dormers in the attic. One-half of the building was used by the fire department, with its two engines.

Paris was seated behind the big, flat desk beside Chief of Police Matt Hruska. Behind them, on the wall, was a large-scale map of the town. Before them on a pad were the notes Paris had made. The Summerton Police Department consisted of a chief and four men. One man was on sick leave. The other three, who included the two day men held over, had been sent to the Summerton Hospital.

The Summerton Hospital had forty beds. Of these thirty-six were occupied. There were nineteen women patients.

Paris studied the notes. One man was dead and a trooper was dying. Lieutenant Joe McKenney had had charge of the case and it had gone badly. Yet he could find no fault with McKenney's operation. McKenney had proceeded as best he could under the circumstances. It was supposed to

68

have been a preliminary meeting. Manpower was always short and, in any event, manpower alone would have been too conspicuous. The use of electronic devices had their place but only in a limited manner. Police work was still a matter of basics: a knowledge of the criminals in your area, the dogged persistence, the legwork, the questioning, and the time spent to winnow out the facts and to obtain evidence. Reliance on the information of the local police department was always the most valuable. Chief Matt Hruska knew his town. He knew Dewey Maddox. According to Hruska, Maddox was a rough, burly man. It was alleged he had beaten up a few people. But he had never killed anyone and had never been known to carry a weapon.

The telephone on the desk rang. Hruska picked it up, spoke, listened, then said, "Wait a minute."

He handed the telephone to Paris. Paris said, "Yes, what is it?" He listened for a moment, then said, "Okay, let me know the minute there's any change."

He put down the telephone. "That was McKenney at the hospital," he said to Hruska. "They're giving Montaigne blood transfusions. No change. He's still on the danger list. The commissioner has sent out a call for more blood."

Hruska nodded dumbly. He took out a cigarette, lighted it, put the burned match down carefully in the half-filled ash tray.

Paris sat still for a moment, looking through the open door of the office across the corridor to another door that was closed. Detective-Sergeant Leonard Small and a state policewoman were sitting in that room with Mrs. Wesley

Cagle. They had been in there for several hours and Mrs. Cagle had refused to answer questions.

He said to Hruska, "Well, Matt, let's try her again."

They got up and went across the hall. When they opened the door Mrs. Cagle was sitting in a chair sipping coffee out of a cardboard cup. Beside her the state policewoman was stirring her own coffee with a small paper spoon. Sergeant Small was standing, leaning against the wall, his hands in his pockets.

Paris sat down at the table beside Mrs. Cagle. He brought out a small revolver. Tied to its trigger was an identification tag. The chrome finish shone brightly in the light of the lamp. The cylinder was now empty. But when the gun had been taken, six cartridges had been ejected from it.

Paris held up the revolver and examined it carefully. It was a Harrington & Richardson—their Guardsman model with a two-and-a-half-inch barrel, six shot, .32 caliber, checkered, red-brown, plastic grips. Probably their Model 633, he thought. The Ballistics Bureau would give him the exact information.

"Now, please, Mrs. Cagle," he said. "Is this gun yours?"

She put her coffee down and compressed her lips. There was no answer. She looked pale and tired.

"It was found in your handbag," Paris said. "We can trace it through its serial number. Just tell us yes or no."

She thought for a moment. "It's mine," she finally said.

"Where did you get it?"

"Wes and I bought it down in Florida."

"When?"

"Three years ago. The summer we drove down there on our vacation."

"Where?"

"At a pawnshop in St. Petersburg. I don't remember the name of it. But the man registered our name."

"Why were you carrying a gun tonight, Mrs. Cagle?"

She sat without answering for a moment. Then she said, "For protection."

"Protection from what?"

"From Dewey Maddox."

"Do you have a license to carry a gun?"

"No."

"If you were so afraid of Dewey Maddox, why did you go to his office tonight?"

"I didn't go to his office."

"Mrs. Cagle," Paris said, "one of our officers saw you hurrying out of the building. The sergeant, here, saw you come home and run into the house. When he came in to pick you up, you tried to hide your handbag. We found the gun in it. We have your identification. We can place you near the scene of the murder."

"It's all a mistake," she said. "A big mistake."

"Well, if it's a big mistake," Paris said, "let's hear why."

"I'm not going to tell you why."

He leaned back in his chair. "Mrs. Cagle, we know all about your husband's debt to Maddox. He told us himself. Aren't you tired of all this?"

"I'm tired," she admitted.

"Then let's get it over with," Paris said. "Why did you go see Dewey Maddox tonight?"

"You know why. Because we owed him the money." Her

face had become less rigid. Her lower lip began to quiver. Suddenly she buried her face in her hands and wept.

They waited silently. The policewoman took a handkerchief from her bag and handed it to Mrs. Cagle. Mrs. Cagle took it and dabbed at her eyes and nose. She drew her breath in deeply. Then she said to Paris, "Dewey threatened to get Wes because of the money."

"We know about that, Mrs. Cagle."

"He threatened to get Wes even in the prison."

"We know that, too, Mrs. Cagle."

"I had to go and plead with him while Wes was away. I had to make sure he didn't carry out the threats."

"Where did you go?"

"To his office," she said, her head down.

"How often?"

"About once a month," she said, dispiritedly.

"Did your husband know?"

"No."

"Does he know now?"

"No, I never told him. I was afraid if he knew, one of them would be killed."

"Why did you go to Maddox's office this particular night?"

"Because I knew something was wrong," she said. "Wes got a call in the afternoon. He went out right after it and didn't get back until late. I knew the call was from Dewey and Dewey wanted his money. So I went to plead with Dewey for more time. I waited until the parole officer came to the house, then I went down to North Main. Dewey's office was closed."

"What time was that?"

"Nine o'clock."

"What did you do then?"

"I went down to the drugstore and called his apartment. There was no answer there. I didn't know what to do. I had a cup of coffee at the drugstore counter and waited. I got to talking with Mr. Simpson, the druggist, and when I looked out the drugstore window again I saw Dewey's car in front of the building."

"What time was that?"

"About twenty minutes past nine."

"What did you do then?"

"I went back there. My car was parked across the street from the building, anyway. I looked up and saw the light in his office. So I opened the downstairs door and climbed the stairs."

"Did you hear anything?" Paris asked.

"I heard Dr. Annis, the dentist. He was working on a patient. His office is two doors away."

"Nothing else?"

"No, I don't think so."

"Did you see anybody?"

"No, sir."

"Go on."

"I came down the corridor. The door to Dewey's office was closed. I turned the knob. It was unlocked. I went inside. Dewey was in his private office on the floor. He was bleeding all over the rug."

"Was he conscious?"

"No. His eyes were closed."

"What did you do then?"

"I called his name softly. He didn't answer. So I ran out.

I went down the stairs, got into my car and drove home. I wasn't in my house but a few minutes when Sergeant Small rang the bell and said he wanted to see me. That was it."

"A gun was found in your bag," Paris said. "Is there any other gun in your house?"

"No."

"We'll have to get a search warrant and look," Paris said.

"You're welcome to do that," she said. "Can I go home now?"

"Not just yet," Paris said.

"When?"

"We'll see."

Paris went out of the room with Sergeant Small and Chief Hruska, taking the revolver and Mrs. Cagle's handbag. The bag would be examined by the chemistry laboratory and the gun by the ballistics laboratory. He envied all those fictional experts who could sniff at a gun barrel and tell if and when it had been fired.

In the Chief's office they set up the tiny, portable tape recorder again. Sergeant Small started the machine. They sat and listened, Paris smoking a cigarette slowly and reflectively. The tape unwound slowly. There was Montaigne's faint voice speaking to the bus driver. Then the sound of his footsteps as he walked, the sound of a car approaching, its motor getting louder. There was Maddox's voice asking who Montaigne was, and there was Montaigne's reply. Then there was the talk and then Montaigne's sketchy description of the third person, and the mention of the woman at the Summerton Hospital.

And there was the sound of three shots, some scuffling noises and the sound of a car driving away. After that, there was the sound of another car approaching and Lieutenant McKenney's voice.

When the recording was stopped, Hruska said, "I recognized Maddox's voice, for sure."

"All right," Paris said. "So we have Montaigne and Maddox. But who was the third party?"

There was no answer because it was not really a question. It was more of a plaintive thought. Hruska rubbed his face and said, "Three shots. Two of them in Montaigne. One in Maddox."

"You mean it all happened at the lake?" Paris asked.

"Three shots," Hruska said. "We heard them on the tape."

"It was dark," Paris said. "All three of them could have been fired at Montaigne. One could have missed. The trouble is there's no evidence that Maddox was shot there. He bled a lot, but it was all in the office. Nothing in the corridor or the outer room. No signs in the car. From the wound he'd have leaked blood freely. Well, we'll wait for the pathologist to tell us," Hruska said.

"Maddox had some girl friends, didn't he?"

"Yes."

"Local?"

"A couple. A waitress over at the Summerton Grill. A girl at the factory. Nothing special. But he did have one in Boston. That one was special."

"Who is she?"

"I never found out who she was."

75

"What about Ducky Britt, his helper? You sure he wouldn't know?"

"You remember we asked him," Hruska said. "I don't think so. I think he was telling the truth when he said Maddox never told him his private business. But we can try him again if you want."

They had questioned Ducky Britt earlier that evening. He had gone to the Gem Theater at 8:00 P.M. and had come out at 11:00 P.M. His mother and sister had been with him.

"Maddox had a lot of enemies," Paris said. "It's going to take a lot of work."

"Half the town are his enemies. I don't know how many will co-operate," Hruska said, looking at him evenly.

It was the old fable of asking which mouse would bell the cat, Paris thought. It was finding someone willing to testify. That was the insidious part of gambling. The respectable citizens looked at gambling tolerantly and fought police investigations all the way. They ignored the bad side effects of criminals in their towns and the corruption they caused.

"The setup was such," Hruska said, "that any man or woman could go into Maddox's office without arousing suspicion. The bank was downstairs. Upstairs was the beauty parlor, the dentist, the lawyer, the loan company and the photography studio." Hruska stood up, pushing his hands deeply into his pockets. "Nobody would talk. Nobody."

Paris saw that Hruska was angry. But the anger was directed toward Hruska himself. A murder had been committed in his town. It was more like a meticulous housewife's finding her immaculate kitchen floor streaked with mud and her walls spattered with ink. It went against Hruska's integrity as a police officer, because the cause and effect of the murder had been there all along and he had been helpless to do anything about it. Paris had known something of it, too. The State Police CIB had kept tabs on Summerton as it had on all towns in the Commonwealth. Of course, there were a few towns and cities where there was a deal between the gamblers and the law. But Summerton was not one of them.

CHAPTER

12

WHEN they came out of the police station the rain was falling. They drove down to the Summerton Hospital. At the hospital entrance there was a roadblock. Two troopers, wearing white luminous crossbelts over their raincoats, stopped them with waving flashlights.

Paris and Hruska drove through into the hospital grounds. The hospital was an old rambling stucco building, two stories high. A smaller, matching building beside it was the nurses' quarters.

When Paris parked the car, Captain Johanssen, commanding Troop A, came over to see him. Johanssen was tall and wide-shouldered. The gold buttons on his dark-blue raincoat gleamed wetly.

"How's Montaigne?" Paris asked him.

"Still alive," Johanssen said. "That's the best I can say."

"How many men do you have here now, Lars?"

"Ten now," Johanssen said.

It was night and they were short on manpower and Paris knew that Johanssen had been squeezed. He probably had had to draw men from as far away as the Topsfield substation. Ten seemed adequate, Paris thought. There was also a state policewoman at the nurses' desk in the women's ward. The hospital, the nurses' quarters and the grounds had been carefully and minutely searched. They had found nothing.

"If you want to see Doctor Zawisza," Captain Johanssen said, "he's in his office."

"Thanks," Paris said.

He stepped out of the car, Chief Hruska following him. The entrance of the hospital had a portico. There was a lighted sign to the left that said AMBULANCE ENTRANCE. Paris walked that way. Beside the ambulance platform there was a door. He opened it.

He was in a corridor smelling of antiseptic. To the right there was a doorway half-shielded with a white cloth screen. Standing in front of it was a uniformed trooper. Beside him stood Detective-Lieutenant Joe McKenney, smoking a cigarette.

Paris came up to him. McKenney pushed the cigarette into a high sand-filled urn. He was haggard, his face heavily lined. He needed a shave.

"How is he?" Paris asked.

"They're giving him blood," McKenney said tonelessly. "He's still unconscious."

"Is it all right for me to go in there?" Paris asked.

"Wait a minute," McKenney said.

He went by the screen and inside. Paris waited. The trooper shifted his feet. McKenney came out.

"All right, Captain," he said.

Paris went by him and into the room. The bed was in

the center. Montaigne lay on his back. His eyes were closed. His head was heavily bandaged. His body was covered with a sheet up to the shoulders. The bed had been slightly elevated so that the head was propped. Above him was a glass bottle of whole blood. It was hooked onto a metal stand with a tube leading down and taped onto his arm. On the other side was another metal stand and a bottle with a colorless liquid in it.

Paris looked at the face. The eyes were closed. The breathing was shallow. The complexion was gray, the face drawn, a dark stubble of beard showing.

Paris turned. On one side, watching him, were three people. One was a doctor in a white coat, a stethoscope hung around his neck. There was a nurse, an older woman with a black band around her white cap and a hospital pin on the breast of her uniform. The third person was a man in a brown business suit, a white shirt and a flowered tie.

He stepped over to Paris and said, "I'm Doctor Zawisza, the head of the hospital. You're Captain Paris?"

"Yes," Paris said. They shook hands.

Paris said, "What are his chances?"

"He's severely wounded," Dr. Zawisza said. "It could go either way."

"He's still unconscious?"

"Yes."

"Do you have any idea when he'll come out of it?"

Zawisza pondered. Paris studied him. The doctor was middle-sized, sandy-haired and blue-eyed. His age seemed to be about forty-five. From his name he was probably of Polish stock.

"There's no telling," Zawisza said. "The bullet hit the side of the head and caused a fracture and some depression of the bone. I'm afraid he'll need surgery. The other wound in the chest is not so serious. It is the head wound."

"We want the best," Paris said.

"Of course," Dr. Zawisza said. "We've called in Borkow from the Massachusetts General. There's none better. He'll be here soon."

"Thanks," Paris said. He could hear the rain dripping from the eaves. "We want this boy. I mean, he's a kid that needs a break. He's had a rough time of it."

He went over to the window and pulled the shade back. Outside he could see a trooper standing motionless in the rain. He turned back to Dr. Zawisza.

"I want this boy to live," he said.

"We do, too," Dr. Zawisza said gently. "Why not come to my office? You'll be more comfortable there, Captain. There's nothing you can do here."

"All right," Paris said.

He went out of there with Dr. Zawisza. In the corridor, Lieutenant McKenney and Chief Matt Hruska joined them. They went down the corridor until they came to the reception desk. An elderly woman sat there near the small switchboard. With her was a trooper.

There was an office door. Above it was a sign that read: *Dr. Valerian Zawisza, Chief of Staff.*

They went in. There was an outer office that held two secretarial desks and a row of leather chairs. The typewriters were hidden by black covers. They went through into another office. Here the curtains on the windows were of bright cretonne. The desk was walnut.

81

"Sit down, gentlemen," Dr. Zawisza said. "Perhaps a drink at this time—"

"No, thank you," Paris said. McKenney shook his head silently.

"How about you, Matt?" Zawisza asked.

"No, thanks, Doc," Hruska said. "I've got a headache."

"We all have," Dr. Zawisza said. He looked around. "Please, sit down, gentlemen."

They sat down. Dr. Zawisza sat down behind his desk. He took up a sheet of paper. "This is the list of women patients that Lieutenant McKenney asked me to prepare," he said. "There are nineteen of them here—eight are maternity cases, two cardiacs and one high blood pressure, two orthopedic cases, a dreadful car accident. One of these women has a compound fracture of the right femur —the big thigh bone—and is in traction. The other has a fracture of the humerus—the upper arm bone—and two fractured ribs. Then we have one hysterectomy—woman's trouble. One ovarian cyst—woman's trouble again. Another is having an exploratory laparotomy—which is a search for a malignancy. We have one breast cancer and two appendectomies." He looked up at them. "That makes a total of nineteen. The Lieutenant has their names and home addresses."

"We would like this kept as quiet as possible," Paris said.

"The hospital concurs exactly," Dr. Zawisza said. He smiled shortly. "There are police at every window and door. The place looks like it's under siege. And you want it kept quiet?"

"We hope to remove most of the police by daylight," Paris said.

"I don't want my patients to become alarmed," Dr. Zawisza said.

"By morning the police won't be very conspicuous," Paris said. "Was Dewey Maddox ever a patient here?"

"No," Dr. Zawisza said.

"You know him?"

"*Of* him," Dr. Zawisza said. "Is he very important to us now?"

"He could have been," Paris said. "He could have told us which woman in your hospital he was trying to get killed."

CHAPTER
13

WADE PARIS was sitting in the outside office of Dr. Valerian Zawisza. It was just past six o'clock in the morning. Through the window he could see the pink sky in the east. The stucco wall of the nurses' home was still in the shadow and some of the lights were on. In front of it a State Police cruiser was parked. A trooper leaned against the door. He could not see the trooper on guard at the rear of the nurses' building but he knew the man was there.

Dr. Zawisza had gone home. Chief Hruska was back in town to begin the tedious task of questioning people. Captain Johanssen had returned to his duties at Troop A Headquarters in Framingham. The state detectives were out working. Six of the troopers had been withdrawn. Now that there was some light, the grounds could be kept under surveillance with fewer men. The six troopers had joined others who were out searching in the Lake Islington area.

Detective-Lieutenant McKenney came in carrying two mugs of coffee. Paris could see the deep, dark circles around his bloodshot eyes and he realized that McKenney had had no sleep for almost twenty-four hours.

He took the coffee with thanks. As he drank, he was thinking that this had been, and still was, McKenney's case. The idea of using the electronic device, the plans for the meet, the tapping of the Cagle telephone were his, Paris', not McKenny's. And Paris would take full responsibility for the failure. That was why he had come so swiftly to Summerton to take charge. Any criticism for bungling should be directed toward him, and that was certain to be.

He drank the coffee absently as he studied the many reports that had come in by now. Trooper Frank Montaigne was still unconscious and in critical condition. He was being prepared for head surgery.

Paris had before him the list of the nineteen female patients at the hospital. Except for the two automobile-accident victims, who were from Ohio, the others were from the Summerton area. The youngest, twenty, was a maternity case. The oldest, seventy-seven, had a cardiac condition and was not expected to live. In an hour they were to be awakened and he would be able to question them. In the meantime they were well guarded.

The nurses and the employees on the night shift had already been questioned. None of them knew Dewey Maddox personally, or Wesley Cagle or Ruth Cagle. None of them had had any dealings with gamblers or knew of anybody who would want to harm them.

Paris read the notes of information that had been telephoned in by Lieutenant Norton from the Ballistics Bureau. The bullet that had been removed from Trooper Montaigne's chest was a .38 caliber. The bullet that had gone into Maddox had passed through and had lodged in the wall behind. This was also a .38 caliber. Tests showed that both bullets had been fired from the same gun.

The gun taken from Mrs. Cagle's handbag was a .32 caliber. A wiping of the barrel and an H acid test showed it had not been fired recently.

The chemistry laboratory had reported that there was no sign of blood in Maddox's car. Information from the State Police pathologist said that no blood had seeped down the body due to gravity. It was apparent that Maddox had been shot and killed in the office where he had been found, and only minutes before Lieutenant McKenney had arrived there.

The dentist, Dr. Annis, had been questioned, as had his patient, a Mrs. William Appleton. Mrs. Appleton had been suffering severe pain from an abscessed tooth and had telephoned Dr. Annis at his home at 8:30 P.M. He had gone immediately to his office in the bank building. Mrs. Appleton arrived five or ten minutes later. Dr. Annis had turned on the radio. He had always felt that music was good therapy. The tooth had been X-rayed and then he had drilled a hole into it to release the gas pressure formed against the nerve. He had not heard any shot from Maddox's office. Neither had Mrs. Appleton. A shot from a .38 made considerable noise. While McKenney stood in the dentist's office, a trooper from the Ballistics Bureau had fired a shot into a barrel of cotton wadding. The radio and the dental drill had been going, but the shot could be heard. This was unsatisfactory to Paris and would have to be investigated further.

Paris turned to McKenney, who was drinking his coffee.

He said, "Joe, when will they have some breakfast ready?"

"In about ten minutes," McKenney said. "I'll skip it. I'm not hungry."

"Better eat," Paris said. The department had a policy that the men ate well the first opportunity they had, because there were times when you went many hours without food. A hungry cop, he knew, was an irritable, impatient and careless cop.

The telephone rang. Paris answered it.

"Wade?" It was Chief Matt Hruska's voice.

"Yes, Matt."

"We've got another death in town."

Paris' throat constricted. "A woman?"

"Yes. Her name's Marie Huntress."

"Where?" He motioned to McKenney to gather up the papers.

"In a rooming house. I'm there now. Sixteen River Street. It's the lower end, down by the river."

"I'll be right over," Paris said. "Is it what I think, Matt?"

"Yes. She'd been working at the Summerton Hospital."

CHAPTER

14

ALONG the curb outside the house was a Summerton police cruiser. A patrolman stood facing the small curious crowd. Some people had gathered in little clusters across the street. Most were wearing bathrobes and coats over their night clothes at this early morning hour. The sun had come up and was casting its first long, slanting rays.

This was the shabby part of Summerton, the mill section, in the bottoms along the river. Most of the houses were over seventy-five years old and had ornate Victorian fronts. There were rows of mustard-colored, wooden frame houses, all alike, close together. Number 16 was larger than the others. It was set back from the street and had a small lawn in front. Perhaps in the past it had been the home of one of the minor mill executives. It was now a boarding house.

Wade Paris went inside with Lieutenant Joe McKenney. In the warm, dimly lit hallway there was an aroma of fresh coffee. There was another door. They opened it and saw Matt Hruska standing in a big, square foyer. With him was an elderly woman with pin curlers in her gray hair, wearing a long, blue, woolen robe. Her eyes were red and she snuffled constantly.

"This is Mrs. Shepper," Hruska said to Paris. "She's the landlady."

Paris took off his hat. It was warm in the house. "Where's the body, Mrs. Shepper?"

"Upstairs," she said. "Matt can show you. I'm not going up there again."

Paris and McKenney followed Hruska up to the second floor. It was the second room on the left. The door was splintered and hung askew on one hinge. There was a sound of water running. Paris glanced at Hruska.

"I got the call about twenty minutes ago," Hruska said. "It was from Mrs. Shepper. She had gone up to see why Mrs. Huntress wasn't up yet. Mrs. Huntress is a maid who works at the Summerton Hospital and she gets up at six. Mrs. Shepper knocked at the door. She could hear water running and there was heat coming out the cracks around the door. When Mrs. Huntress didn't answer, she went down and phoned me. I got here with Bob Foytig, who's down on the sidewalk now. We kicked the door in. It was hot as hell inside. There was a stack hot-water heater burning. We went in to take a look. Then I called you. We touched nothing."

"Let me see," Paris said. He went in by himself. The room was stifling hot. He went quickly to the body on the floor and felt an outstretched wrist. There was no life. The skin was cold and there was no pulse. Rigor mortis had already set in around the face and neck. He got up in a hurry and looked toward the small alcove. There he saw the coil gas heater. Beside it was a hot-water boiler. From a tap below the boiler a rubber hose led to a small white sink. That was where the water was going. Under the sink was a small electric refrigerator. Beside that were a wall cabinet and a small gas stove.

Paris looked at the flame in the gas heater and went rapidly to the window. He hit the glass with his elbow, sharply, breaking the pane and letting in the cool morning air.

Lieutenant McKenney looked into the room.

"Stay there," Paris said. He came out of the room into the hallway. "Carbon monoxide. Phone the gas company and have them send a man to stand by. But first check with Mrs. Shepper to see if the other boarders in the house are all right."

Hruska said, "Anything I can do?"

"Yes, thanks," Paris said. "The medical examiner."

"I already called him," Hruska said. "He'll be here any minute."

"Good," Paris said. "Joe McKenney will call the State Police pathologist, the chem lab and photography. Stick around, Matt. I'll be right out."

Paris went back inside the room. The air was beginning to get cooler. He saw now that it was quite a large room. Beside the alcove there was a closed door. He opened it. It was the bathroom. There was nobody in it. The window was closed and locked.

He came out of the bathroom and looked again at the water heater. In the little cage underneath, the gas flame was ragged and yellow. He straightened up. His eyes moved toward the big window in the room. It was locked and newspapers had been stuffed around the edges. He turned back and looked at the front door. Some of the newspaper wadding around the edge had fallen down when the door had been kicked in. The remainder had been fastened to the edges of the door with cellophane tape. The lock was the automatic, self-locking Yale type. It had been broken.

His eyes swung back to the body which lay on the floor near the stack heater. The face was rigid and expressionless. She wore no cosmetics but the skin had a pinkish tinge. He thought this could be because of the carbon-monoxide poisoning. The eyes were closed. The hair was almost entirely gray but at one time it could have been blonde. She was a middle-aged woman with a broad face and a wide nose. Her body, dressed in a gray skirt and loose gray sweater, was dumpy and almost shapeless. The hands were toil-worn, the fingernails cracked and broken.

He looked at his watch. It was now six-thirty. From what he could see of the body and the hands, the rigor mortis that had set in around the face and neck did not extend to the remainder of the body. It would be hard to estimate the time of death because of the fact that the room had been extremely warm. But she could not have been dead more than four or five hours, which made it a considerable time after the death of Dewey Maddox. He did not see any suicide note.

He went back to the doorway and took another quick glance at the room. With the exception of the shards of glass from the broken window and the rolls of newspaper that had fallen from the door, the room was very clean.

He went out into the hallway and spoke to Hruska. "You didn't see a note, Matt?"

"No," Hruska said.

"Have we got an identification of the woman?"

"Yes. From Mrs. Shepper."

"Okay," Paris said. There was nothing he could do in the room until the medical examiner, the photographers and the chemical laboratory men were through with it.

Lieutenant McKenney came back up the stairs again. He had notified the gas company and the State Police technicians, and had checked to see that the other boarders in the house were in good health. They were.

Paris left him on guard at the door and went downstairs with Chief Matt Hruska. Mrs. Shepper was in a small sitting room on the first floor. The room was somewhat dusty, the windows were grimy and the once-white curtains a dingy gray. There was an odor of mustiness.

"Did you shut off the gas?" she asked Paris.

"No," Paris said. "The man from the gas company will do that. I want my technicians to see that heater first."

"In the meantime we can all die from the gas," Mrs. Shepper said.

"I don't think so," Paris said. "I broke a window in the room. And I believe the gas in Summerton is methane. Is it, Chief?"

"Yes," Hruska said. "All gas in this area is methane. It's nontoxic, Mrs. Shepper. As long as there's air—"

"You mean Mrs. Huntress suffocated?" she asked.

"I don't know yet," Hruska said.

"I don't know either," Paris said. "With the windows all closed, the fire in the stack heater could use up all the oxygen. But if the oxygen was used up, the flame would go out. The flame needs oxygen, too. That flame was burning when Chief Hruska broke open the door. We'll know soon."

"Is it all right for me to smoke?" Mrs. Shepper asked. "I've been dying for a cigarette but I didn't dare."

"Sure," Paris said. He took out a pack of cigarettes and handed her one. He lit it for her. She drew on it deeply.

"Ah," she said. "I needed that." She expelled the smoke. "I'm sorry Chief Hruska had to break that door. It's a good door. I'm insured and I'll collect, but they don't make doors like that any more. I bet a door like that would cost thirty dollars to install."

"Who was Mrs. Huntress?" Paris asked her.

"She was a Polish refugee woman. Very nice and very quiet. Mrs. Huntress spoke hardly any English."

"Do you speak Polish?"

"No," Mrs. Shepper said.

"How did you communicate?"

"Mostly by signs."

"How long had she been here?"

"About seven weeks."

"Where did she come from?"

"Poland."

"Yes, ma'am," Paris said patiently. "But after that. She just didn't walk into this house directly from Poland."

"Oh, no," Mrs. Shepper said. She held her cigarette between her first two fingers. Paris could see they were stained and yellowed. "Mrs. Huntress was sent to me by the Institute for New Americans in Boston. They placed her in the job at the Summerton Hospital and they rented the room for her here." She blew smoke toward the ceiling. "Well, not the room you found her in. She had one of the cheaper rooms on the third floor. But last week she moved to the room she has now."

"Why?"

"Because it has its own bathroom and its own kitchenette, and it's three times bigger, and it's the best apartment in the house."

Paris had noticed she had changed it from *room* to *apartment*. "That must have cost her more money."

"Why, of course. That's a beautiful apartment. It's ninety-five a month, heated and furnished."

"And the other?"

"Fifty a month," Mrs. Shepper said. "I didn't ask her to take the expensive one. She wanted it." Mrs. Shepper frowned. "You're right, Captain. It's kind of strange, isn't it? Almost doubling her rent like that."

"Maybe she had a lot of money," Chief Hruska said.

"I don't think so," Mrs. Shepper said. "How could she? I mean, she didn't have a cent when she got here. I had to wait until she got her first week's pay. She was paying her room rent by the week—one week in arrears. I know she was only getting forty a week as a maid at the hospital. Suddenly last week she paid up her arrears and told me she wanted a better place."

"Maybe she got a raise," Hruska said.

"I found out she didn't."

Paris said, "Who was your contact at the Institute for New Americans?"

"A Mrs. Audrey Crystal. She's the associate director there."

94

Paris wrote it down. "You called the victim *Mrs.* Huntress. Was she married?"

"They told me she'd been married in Poland. She lost her husband. I think they told me it happened a few years back."

"Do you know if Mrs. Huntress was despondent lately?"

"No," Mrs. Shepper said. "Just the opposite. She was all happy and excited."

"About what?"

"I don't know. It started last week when she wanted the bigger apartment. She'd been busy decorating the place, buying fresh flowers. Even singing. Not American songs. Polish, I guess."

"Whom did she know in Summerton?"

"Nobody. I don't know of anybody—unless the head of the hospital, Doctor Zawisza. I can't think of anybody else. Doctor Zawisza is of Polish descent. She worked for him, that's all."

"Has Doctor Zawisza ever been here?"

"I've never seen him."

"Did you ever see Mrs. Huntress with anybody?" Paris asked.

"No. Not here. She never had any visitors."

"How about your other boarders? Did they know her?"

"Just to nod to. She spoke no English."

"Did Mrs. Huntress go out much?"

"No," Mrs. Shepper said.

"Then what did she do with her time?" Chief Hruska asked.

"She usually came right home from work. She'd stay in her room and listen to her radio. She was a person who kept to herself. Once in a while she'd go for a little walk at night. And one Sunday night she went to a dance in Boston."

"When was that?" Paris asked.

"A couple of weeks ago. The Institute sponsored the dance. She got all dressed up. Mrs. Crystal came and called for her in a car."

"Let's take last night," Paris said. "Did you hear anybody go up and visit Mrs. Huntress?"

"No, sir."

"What time did you go to bed, Mrs. Shepper?"

"A quarter-past eleven, right after the news on TV."

"What time did you get up this morning?"

"Half-past five."

"You usually get up at that time?"

"Yes. The older you get, the less sleep you need. I'm always up at five-thirty. Mrs. Huntress usually got up at that time, too. She was due on the job at six."

"And what happened this morning?" Paris asked.

"Mrs. Huntress didn't get up. I waited fifteen minutes and went up to see why. Her door was locked and I heard the water running. I began to pound at the door. She didn't answer. That's when I got frightened. I woke up everybody else in the house."

"Who?"

"Mr. O'Brien first. He works at the mill. We thought maybe there was something wrong with the gas. So he woke everybody else. That was Miss Hubbard, Miss Kantor and Mrs. Armbreister."

"Who has the room next to Mrs. Huntress?"

"Mr. O'Brien. He's the one who called the police."

"Thank you, Mrs. Shepper," Paris said.

He stood up. He was very tired. His eyes were heavy and itching. He knew his efficiency would be impaired unless he got at least a few hours' sleep. McKenney and the others would need rest, too. He would wait for the medical examiner and the technicians to arrive; then he would call in Detective-Lieutenant Mike Barney to take charge for the time being.

CHAPTER

15

Paris was awakened by the sound of the telephone ringing. He looked at the electric clock on the night table beside his bed. It was twenty minutes past noon. He picked up the receiver and said hello. It was the commissioner's secretary. She asked if he would speak with the commissioner. He would.

The commissioner came on. He was succinct and to the point. The brain operation on Trooper Frank Montaigne had been successful. They had cut through the temporal bone and a blood clot had been removed from the brain. However Montaigne had not yet regained consciousness and was still in serious condition.

The commissioner then said he was sorry that the case had been so badly botched. A trooper had been seriously wounded. One man had been murdered. Then a woman in Summerton had been found dead under suspicious circumstances. This had all happened in an area that was supposedly surrounded and controlled by the police. The commissioner would appreciate an explanation. Not only were the newspapers insistent, but the state senator from the Summerton district had been asking some pertinent questions from the capitol on Beacon Hill.

Paris said he would be at State Police Headquarters in half an hour. He hung up and telephoned the Summerton Hospital. Frank Montaigne had improved. His pulse and respiration were better and he now showed signs of awakening. He called the Summerton Police Headquarters and reached Detective-Lieutenant Mike Barney. They had been holding Mrs. Ruth Cagle on the charge of carrying a concealed weapon, but her attorney had posted bail for her and she had been released.

"I've got her under surveillance though," Barney said.

"Who's doing it?" Paris asked.

"I brought in Sergeant Roy Harnish," Barney said.

"Anybody else around?"

"Ed Styman's at the hospital," Barney said. "I've borrowed a trooper for the boarding house. Did you hear that Montaigne's better?"

"Yes," Paris said. "Has McKenney called?"

"He's coming in," Barney said. "And I just heard from Walt Franz. He'll be here in twenty minutes. Anything else, Captain?"

"Stay there with McKenney," Paris said. "I'll be out as soon as I can."

"Will do," Barney said.

Paris hung up the phone and went in to take his shower. When he came out into the living room he looked out the window and saw the bright flowers and the greenery of the Public Garden. The swan boats were in use.

The commissioner was right, he thought. On the face of

it, the case had gone very badly. With the prior information and preparation, they should have had better results. Perhaps he should have tried to use more men. But to use more men meant taking them off some other important job. There were just so many men you could use, anyway. To have brought more men and vehicles into the Lake Islington area would have attracted attention and could have frightened away the quarry. In his judgment it had been best to keep contact with the electronic device. The trooper, Frank Montaigne, had been the decoy. Of necessity, he had to be unarmed. Troopers and young detectives who did undercover work were usually unarmed and carried either fake identification papers or no papers at all. If they worked among narcotic pushers, prostitutes, petty gamblers and car thieves, they were usually unshaven and ragged-looking, too. That was part of the blending in of a detective with the particular environment. That was normal procedure.

He thought of the protective provisions that had been put in order. This had been the first meeting between Maddox and the supposedly hired killer. According to prior experience such meetings were always exploratory. For anyone to shoot a complete stranger like Frank Montaigne alias Jack Barr was completely illogical. They had checked both Barr and Montaigne carefully. Neither had ever been in the Summerton area or known people in it. McKenney had had a man watching Maddox's apartment and he had noted that Maddox had left there at 8:00 P.M. Sergeant Small had watched the Cagle house and had seen Mrs. Cagle leave and return. The Summerton night-route officer had checked the Maddox office building in his cruiser. He had gone by at 8:45 P.M. and had noted that the office was dark. But he had a large area to cover and from nine until nine-thirty he had been at the other end of Summerton toward the Lake Islington area. The office was not considered very important because Maddox rarely used it at night. Because there were several roads leading from Lake Islington, the night officer had missed Maddox's green car returning. That was it. It was entirely unexpected that Maddox, himself, would be a victim.

As for the death of Mrs. Marie Huntress, that was a question of the timing. Her death had not been on the hospital grounds. Technically she did fit Maddox's category as "a woman at the Summerton Hospital." But it had been necessary to check out each of the female patients first. Then the nurses, the physiotherapists, the laboratory technicians and the office staff. The female population at the Summerton Hospital had been checked in order of their importance. The menial and custodial help were, naturally, of less importance and immediacy. By noon of that day they would have come to Marie Huntress. But that would have been too late. It was that kind of case, he thought. The kind where you did everything right, but you were always too late and always one step behind.

When he arrived at State Police Headquarters he went directly to the commissioner's private office. The talk was quiet and restrained. They went over the case step by step. There was no admissible error. To have tailed Maddox from his apartment might have alerted him. They lacked evidence and could not have taken him into custody.

But what was done could not be undone. The commissioner knew it. Wade Paris knew it. The newspapers were insistent and politicians had to be assuaged. There were no explanations and no announcement of arrests "to be expected shortly." A hundred troopers had volunteered as blood donors for Montaigne. That was all they had for the press.

Paris shook hands with the commissioner, picked up his hat and drove back to his office. His desk was covered with paper slips. He glanced at the top one and picked up the phone and dialed the State Police pathologist. The autopsy of Dewey Maddox, he was told, had been completed. Death had been caused by a bullet passing upward through the stomach and bursting through the heart. The entrance wound was larger than the exit, a result probably of the gas pressure of the blast. The murder weapon had been fired at extremely close range. The muzzle of the gun had apparently been pushed hard into the victim's clothing at the time of the shot.

The autopsy of Marie Huntress was not yet complete. She had apparently suffered a blow on the head before death. There was a laceration on the scalp that could have been caused by a gun butt. But death itself had been caused by monoxide poisoning.

Paris thanked the doctor, pushed down the receiver and phoned the chemistry laboratory. He was told that there were powder burns on Dewey Maddox's clothing. The shot had singed the shirt material, and this confirmed the findings of the autopsy report.

He called up to the fourth floor and spoke with the supervisor of ballistics. Lieutenant Philip Norton was a young man, very quick and intelligent. His work was well respected by every member of the force.

"There were two people two doors away from Maddox's office," Paris said to Norton. "If a shot was fired they should have heard it."

"Maybe not," Norton said. "There was a case out in the Midwest something like this. The muzzle of the gun was wrapped around the victim's clothing and the barrel pressed hard into the flesh. When the gun went off the gases and shock waves were contained in the body. The whole thing happened in the living room of a boarding house. There were ten people in the adjacent dining room eating supper. All right, people were talking and there was the clink of china and silverware. But nobody heard anything. There wasn't even a doorway between the rooms. Just an archway. Well, we tried the experiment here in the lab. No matter how we wrapped the barrel and fired it into cotton waste we got noise. A pronounced shot, even with a silencer."

"Maybe if it was a body—"

"I was going to say that, Captain. Maybe if we experimented with a live animal we could tell. It's possible. I know there's pressure on you—"

"Thanks, Phil," Paris said. He hung up and absently poked through the scattered notes and memorandums on his desk. He rifled through his desk drawer and carefully sharpened three yellow pencils. He pushed them into his inside coat pocket, turned in his swivel chair and frowned through the window for several minutes. Then he picked up his hat and went out of the office.

CHAPTER
16

Paris drove into Summerton and went directly to the Shepper boarding house. There was a uniformed trooper at the front door, and the usual knot of curiosity seekers. And several newspapermen too, for some camera bulbs flashed as he stepped from his car.

He went up to Mrs. Huntress's room and found Joe McKenney standing near the window, one foot on the radiator, smoking a pipe. Near him on the floor were neat piles of clothing, jewelry and documents.

McKenney said, "You got the report from the M.E.?"

Paris turned and looked at the splintered door. It bothered him. "Yes," he said. He went over and squinted at the rolls of newspaper fastened to the edges with long, neat strips of cellophane tape.

"All right. So she died of gas poisoning," McKenney said. "But she was hit on the head first."

"Maybe," said Paris. He ran his finger along the cracked doorjamb. "She might have fallen and hit her head on the stove, too."

McKenney shrugged. "Could be, Captain. But I don't think so," he said. He pressed a smooth wooden tamp into the bowl of his pipe and looked at Paris closely. Paris seemed a comparatively young man, but the hard lines etched around his eyes and the corners of his mouth told a different story—the story of a man governed for many years by a deep, rigid discipline. The years of strain and tension had left their mark. Old Icewater, they called him. But it was always said with respect. For though he demanded a great deal from his subordinates, he would always back them up if he felt they were right. And if a case had gone badly, as this one certainly had, and if it was not the fault of his subordinates, Paris would take the blame.

"Why don't you think so?" Paris was asking.

"The whole thing smells of rigging. The front door and the windows were all locked. Every crack was stuffed with newspapers."

"Normal suicide procedure," Paris said. "Go ahead."

"Then why were the newspapers around the front door attached with tape? Why wouldn't she have taped the papers to the windows as well? Or the bathroom door?" He turned and looked through the window down onto the street below. By now most of the crowd had wandered off although several men with press cameras still lingered by the front steps. "And why no suicide note?"

"About the suicide note," said Paris, "that's not always true. In this case she was Polish and couldn't write in English. She probably thought if she wrote a note nobody could have read it anyway. But you're right about the door. That's the only place where the tape was used." He frowned. "Airtight," he said. "It could have been shut and locked from the outside. No hard job when there's an automatic lock like this."

McKenney said, "The murderer could have hit Mrs. Huntress on the head, stuffed paper along the cracks of the windows and sealed the bathroom door. Then he taped the newspapers around the edges of the front door and turned on the gas jets. He opened the front door and slammed it shut from the hallway. The automatic lock snaps in and the room is sealed up tighter than a drum." He drew thoughtfully on his pipe. "What other reason could there be for taping papers around the front door and not anywhere else?"

"I'll buy that," Paris said. He walked across the room and bent over the neat pile of clothing.

"You've seen this?" he asked McKenney. He lifted up a pale blue and gray cocktail dress and thumbed back the collar. "The labels?"

"Bonwit Teller," McKenney said. "There are a couple more from Cyreld's in Brookline. They're all from fancy stores. Take a look at the shoes. Five pairs of them. An I. Miller stamp inside every one of them."

"Her pay scale was a dollar plus one meal. Forty-hour week. Less Blue Cross and deductions. About thirty-four dollars net."

"You ought to see the groceries in the kitchen cabinet. She's a gourmet. All S.S. Pierce stuff."

"She was paying ninety-five dollars a month rent on thirty-four dollars take-home pay. Her clothes are the best and yet she worked as a scrubwoman in the hospital. Did you find any money around?"

McKenney shook his head. "No," he said. "Her purse was empty except for a few coins." He had, of course, looked to see if anything had been taped under the bathroom sink or in the bathroom flush tank. He had gone over every part of the bed and had pulled the pictures off the wall in case anything had been pasted behind them. He had looked behind the mirrors and dug through the window box. People could think of a lot of places where they felt their valuables could be safely hidden.

Paris stood up and looked around the room. He could see the smears of black powder where the technicians had dusted, looking for fingerprints. As yet their report hadn't come in.

He bent over the piles again and plucked up a large Manila envelope. It was sealed with two short strips of cellophane tape. He eyed the envelope thoughtfully and then went over to the studio bed and sat down. He reached into his pocket, pulled out a small black penknife and carefully cut through the outer flap. Inside he found an alien registration card from the Department of Justice, Immigration and Naturalization Service. The card carried the name of Marie Huntress in neat, black type. It said that she was forty-five years old and had been born in the town of Susz, Poland. The port of entry had been New York City and had been stamped seven weeks before. He pulled out a carbon copy of a letter from Audrey Crystal of the Institute for New Americans to Dr. Valerian Zawisza of the Summerton Hospital, explaining that Mrs. Huntress spoke no English but that she was a good worker and they thought she would be better placed at the Summerton Hospital since Dr. Zawisza had a knowledge of the Polish language.

All right, thought Paris. What now? Here was a woman who had been in the country only seven short weeks. Apparently she had associated with nobody in Summerton. And now she was gone. He studied the face on the alien registration card. It was a plain face. A face that looked back at him impassively. Almost indifferently. He said, "Huntress is an odd name. Could it be Polish?"

McKenney sat down on the studio bed beside him. "Doesn't sound like it," he said. "Sounds too Anglicized."

A notebook had been recovered from Dewey Maddox's flat. In it were a hundred names of people in the Summerton area. Beside each name were various marks, triangles, dots, squares and stars. It was some kind of code, but they would be able to break it easily enough at GHQ. Yet it gave them a hundred additional people to check out. Cagle's name was on the list, and his brother-in-law, Alfred Weaver. Different symbols were beside the names.

"At the hospital," McKenney said, "quite a few of the patients had heard of Maddox. But not one said she knew him personally."

"Any of their names in the notebook?"

"No," McKenney said. "One nurse knew him, though. She went out with him a couple of months ago." He glanced at Paris. "Her alibi checks out for last night, though," he added. "She was on duty."

Paris looked down at the picture of Marie Huntress again and then carefully slid it back into the Manila envelope. "We'll have some pictures made of this woman. Show them around the area, the bars, the stores, anywhere else she might have gone. Find out if Maddox knew her, and why."

"Doesn't seem likely." McKenney smiled. "Matt Hruska told me Maddox liked them younger and more shapely."

"Maybe he did," Paris said. "But I still think this was the woman Dewey Maddox wanted murdered."

"Could be. And could be that Dewey Maddox was only the middleman for somebody else who wanted her murdered."

Paris grunted. "Not any more he isn't," he said.

They both looked up at a light knock from the apartment doorway. Sergeant Styman leaned in and said, "Captain?"

"Yes?"

"Frank Montaigne is conscious."

Doctor Zawisza stood for a moment, his chin cupped in his hand. "He's badly wounded, Captain," he said. "It could go either way."

"He is conscious, isn't he?" Paris asked.

"Yes."

"May I talk with him?"

Zawisza pondered for a moment. Then he picked up the telephone and spoke into it. When he put the phone down he said, "You can see him for a few minutes. Naturally, I don't have to warn a man of your experience, Captain. He's very ill. The slightest—"

"I understand," Paris said. "He's one of ours. I'll be very brief."

They went out of the office and started down the white corridor. They turned right and came to a room with the door standing ajar. A state trooper and a Summerton policeman were standing outside it. Paris took a quick look inside. He saw a white portable screen and a doctor in a white coat with a stethoscope around his neck talking with a gray-haired nurse.

In a moment the nurse came out and nodded briefly to Doctor Zawisza. Zawisza turned to Paris and said, "It's all right to go in now. But do make it as brief as possible."

"Of course," said Paris. He entered the room. Montaigne was on his back. He looked very pale, and the stubble of his beard showed sharply against his chin.

Paris sat down in a chair and took out his notebook. "Do you know me, Montaigne?" he said.

"Yes, sir," Montaigne whispered. "Captain Paris."

"Good. Who shot you?"

"I don't know."

"You were talking to Maddox. He asked you to kill a woman at the Summerton Hospital. What happened then, Frank?"

"Somebody else was there. He was wearing a dark suit and a black stocking over his face as a mask."

"Did he talk to you?"

"No, sir." Montaigne paused for a moment. He drew a deep breath and Paris waited. "I tried to get him to talk so his voice would be on the tape recorder. He wouldn't talk. He pushed Maddox away and pulled out a gun and shot me."

"What happened then?"

"I don't know. There was an explosion in my head and I blacked out. Next thing I knew I was here."

"This person didn't say a word?"

"No, Captain."

"Can you give me a description?"

"Medium height, about five seven or eight. Dark clothes. Medium build. Not fat, not too thin. In the dark it was hard to tell."

"The weapon?"

"A revolver. That's all I saw."

"Barrel?"

"I don't know, sir. I couldn't see. Four-inch maybe."

"And this masked person knew Maddox?"

"Yes, sir. He was there beside Maddox—" He stopped suddenly and cupped his eyes with the palms of his hands. "Look, Captain. I've got a little girl at home. I don't want her to know I'm hurt bad. Would you call my mother and ask her to take care of—"

"Sure," Paris said.

"Little kids are scared of these things."

"Sure," Paris said.

"I'm sorry I bungled the job, Captain."

"You did a fine job, Frank. It just didn't work out."

"Did you get Maddox?"

Paris climbed to his feet and put his hand on the trooper's arm. "Yeah, Frank," he said. "We've got him."

"Good. I'm glad you have."

"I'm going now, boy," said Paris quietly. "You take care of yourself. You're going to be in damn fine shape in another week or two."

Montaigne managed a weak grin. "I know I will, Captain. I've just got to be, that's all."

CHAPTER
17

THE Institute for New Americans was on Commonwealth Avenue in the Back Bay section of Boston. It was an old brownstone building, four stories high. Paris went up the wide, gracefully curving staircase to the second floor. The room he entered was spacious and high ceilinged. In the back was a pair of French windows that led out onto a balcony. White floor-length curtains rustled softly in the breeze.

The room was dominated by a row of plain, gray filing cabinets and two flat mahogany desks. Behind one of them sat a slim, well-groomed and pretty woman. She wore a gray sharkskin suit and a white lace-collared blouse. Her black hair was curled around her head in a bubble cut. She stood up when Paris came in and extended her hand.

"Captain Paris?" she asked. Her grip was firm and warm. Paris judged her to be in her late twenties.

"Yes."

"I'm Audrey Crystal, the associate director." She motioned to a chair by her desk. "Please sit down, Captain.

I'm sorry our director, Doctor Fritz Raeder, is not here to meet you. He's out at a meeting with a few other Red-Feather agencies. But he should be back shortly. Cigarette?"

She extended a small teakwood box. He took one. She took one herself and he lit it for her. She said, "In the meantime, if there is anything I can do—"

"It's about Marie Huntress."

"Yes," she said slowly. "I thought it would be when I heard you were coming. I read about her death in the early afternoon editions. I'm terribly shocked." She tapped her cigarette ash into a large green glass ash tray. "Everybody here is shocked. That it could happen to one of ours. It's the first time that anything like this has happened to us."

Paris nodded. "What did you know of her?"

"Well, I think I knew her more than anyone else in the Institute. When Mrs. Huntress came here, Doctor Raeder was on vacation in Florida. Naturally I took charge and processed her. That was almost two months ago. Around the middle of April, I think."

"Do you have a file on her?"

"Of course. Excuse me, I'll get it." She stood up and Paris smiled as he watched her walk across the room to the filing cabinets. Mrs. Crystal had nice legs.

She came back with a tan cardboard folder and sat down. "Here we are," she said. "Marie Huntress. Native of Susz, Poland." She tapped the folder lightly on the desktop and managed a grim smile. "She was one of the luckier ones who managed to escape the Communist Utopia."

"Up until last night she was."

"Yes, of course."

Paris leaned forward. "How do they do it? I've heard the Iron Curtain is a pretty tough thing to get through."

"How?" She turned the folder around until the edge lay parallel to the bottom of the desk. She studied it thoughtfully. "Oh, there are many ways to escape from behind the Iron Curtain. They bribe their way through, traveling at night and sleeping and hiding during the day. She got into East Germany, stayed there awhile, and then slipped into the American sector in West Berlin. There she asked for admittance into the United States."

"Is there a quota?"

"Oh, yes. It's around sixty-four hundred. That's the Polish quota, of course. It all depends upon the country of your birth, not the country you come through. Czechs, Hungarians, Poles, most of them come through East Germany into West Berlin."

"Where do you put all the people?"

"The West German welfare agencies provide for them. There's the Marienfelde Refugee Camp in West Berlin, although it's not really a camp as we would describe it. It's more like a big apartment house, completely surrounded by a high wire fence."

"Have you been there?"

"I took a trip there last summer."

"Why the fence?"

"Oh, not to keep the refugees in. The fence is for their protection. As you know, Berlin is a free-access city. The Communists can roam through the Western sector with little if any difficulty at all."

"Looking for trouble?"

"Exactly." She paused. "Mrs. Huntress was at that camp."

"How did she come here?"

"First she applied for a visa from the U.S. Consul in Bonn to enter under the Polish quota. All of them don't apply for an American visa, of course. Some have relatives who have preceded them to Canada or South American countries."

"Did she have any relatives here?" Paris asked. "In this country?"

"No. Nobody. But she wanted to come here. So, she had her physical. The State Department makes sure that the migrant has no loathsome or contagious disease, no insanity, no tuberculosis. And they can't become an economic risk either. In other words, Marie Huntress couldn't come to the States without a guarantee of employment. And that's where we come in. We guarantee the Immigration and Naturalization Service that the migrant won't be a burden. We are able to place these people in jobs, mostly as service workers in hospitals and institutions as maids, dishwashers and porters. There's always a shortage of those and they don't have to know English. You must understand that even the well-educated migrants must take some kind of work before they're allowed entry. Marie Huntress was an educated woman."

"But no knowledge of English."

"No. French, German and Russian. But no English. She and her husband were both schoolteachers in Poland."

Paris pulled out a small, black, leather notebook. "What happened to her husband?" he said.

"At the start of the war he was with the Polish Army.

He was captured soon afterward and put into a slave labor camp. After the armistice he returned to Susz. But things weren't much better under the Communist rule, so he fled to the West. He was reported killed trying to cross the border. There were no children. Her relatives all died in labor camps during the war. They were in either German or Russian camps. They either died by disease or starvation." She reached out and pushed the folder to one side. "Or by execution," she added.

"She had no love for the Russians then?"

"Hardly. From what I can understand she was a member of some resistance group during the war. Then the Russians took over her country and put in a puppet government and it was the same thing all over again." Audrey Crystal sighed. "It's such a common story with our migrants that sometimes I feel like I'm a phonograph needle stuck in a groove."

"I'd like to know if she came to this country alone," Paris said.

"Entirely alone. I remember her coming into South Station on the train from New York. The Travelers Aid had put her on the train in Grand Central and told her to stay until the end of the line. I was at South Station to meet her myself. I brought her to the Institute here to freshen up. We had some tea and we had an orientation talk. She was shabby, ill dressed and, of course, rather frightened. As you or I would be in a strange land with a strange language."

"How did you talk with her?"

"We have volunteers. There was a fine woman here, a Mrs. Marsha Copel, who served as interpreter. There was really nothing special to talk about. She had come through the usual routine. I remember it well from personal experience."

Audrey Crystal sat back and smoked her cigarette and told Paris of the long, patient queues of ill-clad people in Berlin who stood and waited to be interrogated and who were assigned to dormitories at Marienfelde. At Marienfelde they were processed. They were given their plane tickets and flown to hostels, usually in Bonn in West Germany. From there they were sent to Hamburg or Bremerhaven and transported out of Germany by ship. Not first class, but not steerage either, like in the pre-World War I days. The ICEM provided for their transportation.

"The what?" Paris asked, his pencil poised.

Mrs. Crystal smiled. "The Intergovernmental Committee for European Migration. I'm sorry, Captain. I'm so accustomed to these alphabetical organizations. On arrival at New York Mrs. Huntress made a declaration of obtaining citizenship. It meant of course she would have to go to school to learn to read and write and speak English. We arrange for night school for them. We do what we can. But we have very limited funds."

"What about other Polish people here?"

"We try to get them to join ethnic groups. The Polish Cultural Society is one. They had a dance here last week."

"How often do they meet?"

"Every week. Upstairs. Mrs. Huntress was at the dance they held two weeks ago."

Paris looked up. "How often did she attend these dances?"

"That dance was her first time. She seemed very happy. Why do you ask?"

"It's always possible that Mrs. Huntress had been busy in a Communist resistance group and had been followed to this country."

"Yes, that's possible." Audrey Crystal puckered her lips into a small, tight O and then said, "She was a placid person. I don't quite believe she could have been very active along those lines. Still you might be able to find that out from the State Department. The C.I.A., I think it is."

"It's also possible that somebody in the Polish Cultural Society knew her and passed the word along."

"Such a thing is possible. I suppose you'll want a list of all the members."

"Yes, please. I'm not one who looks for goblins, Miss Crystal. But we have to examine every contingency."

"I understand. As a matter of fact, Mrs. Huntress was reluctant to join the group. It's very common, of course. They're fearful of joining anything. They've been going through security clearances in Europe on subversive organizations. They'd rather be on the safe side and not join anything. We have to explain to them that we have no subversive clubs here at the Institute."

"Can you tell me anything about the dance two weeks ago? We know so little about this woman."

"What can I tell you, Captain? I didn't pay much attention to her. It was a busy evening. I did notice that she came in and she danced with one or two of the men. She seemed to be having a good time. Otherwise she was quite undistinguished. No man showed any great interest in her."

"How was she dressed?"

"Rather poorly."

"Was she wearing a black cocktail dress? Or a blue and gray one?"

"No. It was print cotton."

"Jewelry?"

"I didn't notice anything."

"Shoes?"

"I didn't notice. That's about all I know. She took the late bus back to Summerton. And that's the last I saw of her. Two weeks ago."

Paris sat up and looked at Audrey Crystal. Her slender hands were folded neatly on the desk. The slim fingers were interlaced and her trim, manicured fingernails were scarlet against the white of her hands. "How about the name?" he said. "Huntress. It's not a Polish name, is it?"

"No. She had a rather long and difficult name. They changed it in Germany. You can check it if you want. Her original name is on file with the State Department. Perhaps it might mean something."

He made a note. "Probably not."

"It should be on her passport."

"We couldn't find it."

Audrey Crystal said, "Oh."

"Would you have it here?"

"No. Perhaps you could find out more from Doctor Raeder, our director. He speaks Polish as well as several other languages. As I remember I saw him talking to Mrs. Huntress at the dance. And quite earnestly. I'm sure he'll remember her."

"How about the doctor at the Summerton Hospital. Was he at the dance?"

"Doctor Zawisza? Yes, he was. He danced with Mrs. Huntress. A wonderful man. He's Polish-American and speaks Polish very fluently. That's why we send him many Polish refugees. He has great sympathy and compassion for them."

"Thank you," Paris said. Mrs. Audrey Crystal, he thought. Probably widowed or divorced. He looked again at the ring finger of her left hand. It was bare.

She noticed his glance. "My husband was an Air Force pilot. He was in Korea."

"I'm very sorry," Paris said.

"It's quite all right. He wasn't killed. He met a girl in Japan. A WAF officer. She was available. I wasn't. They fell in love while he was on leave. I was young then and it's been some years now. Are you married, Captain?"

"No," he said.

She looked at his short-clipped sandy hair, the lean, tanned face and the crinkles around his pale blue eyes. He had a strong mouth, she thought. And there was an air of competence about him.

"Do you find it lonely?" she asked.

Paris smiled. "Yes, I do," he said. "Don't you?"

"Yes," she said. "I wouldn't have minded so much if there'd been a child. The work is compensating. But it's not enough." She turned slightly in her chair and folded her hands neatly in her lap. "How is that trooper who was shot?"

"He's coming along," Paris said. "Do you ever get to Summerton?"

"Not often."

"Would you like to?"

"Why?"

"I thought you might like to visit him," he said. "He's a widower. He has a small daughter—"

"Poor child," she said, and then suddenly her expression changed. "If that isn't the most flagrant kind of matchmaking!" She laughed.

Paris grinned. "He's a nice boy and you seem to be a nice girl—"

He heard a door open and he turned. It was the door of a self-service elevator. The door clanged shut, and a man came striding into the room. He was tall, thin and very erect. He wore a gray, pencil-striped suit. His dark glossy hair was combed back past distinguished silvery temples. Paris stood up.

"Audrey?" the man asked.

"Yes, Doctor," she said. She stood up and two red spots showed high on her cheeks. "This is Captain Paris, Chief of Detectives, State Police. Captain, Doctor Raeder."

"Oh, yes," Raeder said. He gripped Paris' hand. A strikingly handsome man, Paris thought. A thin-lipped mouth, blue eyes, narrow aristocratic nose. His suit, Paris knew, was hand tailored. The accent sounded North European, but Paris couldn't be sure.

Dr. Raeder said, "I presume that this is about the unfortunate death of Mrs. Huntress." He was moving toward the other large desk in the room.

Paris followed him. "Yes," he said.

Raeder took out a flat gold cigarette case and offered a cigarette to Paris. Paris shook his head.

"It is unfortunate," Raeder said standing behind the desk. He frowned and tapped the cigarette on the case. "Have you discovered the reason for the suicide? Did she leave a note of explanation, perhaps?"

"We're not of the opinion it was suicide," Paris said.

"Oh," Raeder said, frowning again. "One of *those* things."

Audrey Crystal came toward them. "If you wish to talk, Doctor," she said, "I'll be downstairs."

"Thank you, Audrey," Raeder said.

To Paris she said, "I'll be waiting on the first floor if you want to ask me any more questions, Captain."

"Thank you," Paris said. "That will be fine."

She walked away toward the staircase, her slim, high heels tapping across the polished, inlaid floor. Paris had noticed the way her cheeks had colored and the way her eyes had been fixed on Raeder. But Raeder had seemed indifferent. Almost distantly amused.

"You're the Chief of Detectives?" Raeder asked.

"Yes."

"You usually do this? Interview people? Make inquiries?"

"No, not usually."

"Then it must be an important case to you."

"It is," Paris said. "For a number of reasons. Mrs. Huntress is important. But she is only part of the case."

"And just exactly what can I do for you, Captain?" Raeder said, easing himself into the large, high-backed chair behind the desk. "Please sit down, Captain," he said. "Make yourself comfortable."

122

Paris sat down and said, "How well did you know Mrs. Huntress?"

"I met Mrs. Huntress once," he said. "I was away on vacation when she first came through our Institute. Two weeks ago there was a dance of the Polish Cultural Society. She was there. It seemed she came from the village of Susz in western Poland. I was born in Germany, not far from there—Mecklenburg near the Baltic."

"Huntress is an odd name for a Pole, isn't it?"

Raeder smiled and spread his hands. "I'm sorry. I'm not too familiar with Polish names."

"Have you been in this country long, Doctor?"

"Over thirteen years. I studied sociology and psychology in Vienna. Then I came to this country and received my Ph.D. at the University of Southern California. That is where I met my wife. She was attending lectures there." He smiled again. "But I'm sure you are not interested in my personal life, Captain. It is Mrs. Huntress you wish to know about. I'll get her file."

"It's on Mrs. Crystal's desk."

"Then you've seen it?"

"Yes." Raeder went over and picked up the file. He came back, absently shuffling through the papers. Paris said, "You spoke to Mrs. Huntress two weeks ago."

"Was it two weeks ago?"

"The dance of the Polish Cultural Society."

"Of course. I'm sorry, but we have so many ethnic groups here that it is very hard to keep them all straight. Yes, I do remember speaking with Mrs. Huntress."

"About what, Doctor?"

Raeder pressed his finger tips together. "Hmmm. Yes,

now I remember. She was working at a hospital. We have many migrants working at hospitals. This was Summerton, wasn't it?"

"Yes," Paris said.

"Summerton. That's Doctor Zawisza. He's of Polish descent." Raeder leaned back and drew on his cigarette. He blew a tight, blue stream of smoke toward the ceiling and smiled thoughtfully. "A very nice chap, Zawisza. But not on the same social level as Mrs. Huntress. Not at all. Mrs. Huntress had problems."

"What kind?" Paris asked.

"She was unhappy in Summerton. She asked if I could find her a position elsewhere. She wanted to be with more people of her age and kind. I promised to do what I could. In fact I have a memorandum of it somewhere. I do the best I can for these people. That was the extent of my conversation with Mrs. Huntress."

"Did she say anything about her background?" Paris asked.

"Her background?"

"Can we discount the fact that she might have been killed for political reasons?"

"I see what you mean," Raeder said. "I'm an American citizen now. But I've had experience with the Communists. I was in the German Army. When I returned to Mecklenburg it was occupied by the Russians. My family was gone. They made life quite untenable for us."

Paris said, "You escaped from behind the Iron Curtain?"

"Well, not exactly escaped," Raeder said. "You might say that I got quite lucky. What we call a section six. These are escapees. Displaced persons, people in exile, things like that." Raeder smiled. "They still might have families in their country of origin. If they do, they might fear physical or political or religious persecution for their loved ones. But they all come under the Displaced Persons Act."

"I see." Paris leaned back and a flutter of white caught the corner of his eye. A gust of wind had snatched at the curtains by the French windows. But now they lay still against the wall. "And you entered the country in the same way, Doctor?"

"No. I entered under the auspices of an exchange scholarship." He looked over Paris' shoulder and frowned. "Now as I say, she might have been a part of some anti-Communist group. It's not illogical. She might have been in physical danger and fled for her life. They have been known to follow people all over the world. If you will remember they murdered Trotsky in his Mexican asylum."

"She hardly looked like a political leader," Paris said. "Did she mention anything about this to you?"

"No," Raeder said. "But she could have been in possession of important information or even a courier perhaps. These undistinguished people make the best couriers. She wouldn't say anything about it, of course. Naturally she'd be afraid. Being in this country for such a short time and not knowing anything."

"So you knew nothing about her of your own knowledge?"

"No."

"Did she express any kind of fear to you?"

Raeder looked at the tip of his cigarette. "In a way— but very vaguely. She said she was afraid of being in Summerton. She said she was all alone there. She knew nobody. She wanted to get into another, larger area where she could mingle with more people her kind. At the time I thought it was just a routine complaint."

"Did she mention anybody by the name of Dewey Maddox to you?"

"No."

"Wesley Cagle?"

"No. I don't recall that she mentioned any names. This Maddox was the criminal that was killed last night?"

"Yes."

"Was he a native-born American?"

Paris answered, "Yes."

"Of course, that doesn't signify anything," said Raeder. "These people do have some native Americans on their pay rolls. But she never did mention anybody."

"Thank you," Paris said, standing up.

"I wish I could have been more help," Raeder said. "I feel a sense of responsibility for these migrants."

"You've done very well," Paris said.

Raeder said, "Call on me any time."

They shook hands and Paris left the room, taking the wide-sweeping staircase to the first floor. The building, he thought, had once belonged to one of the prominent Boston merchant families. They had since moved out to Dover, Weston, Lincoln, Dedham or Wellesley Hills. The old homes were now taken over by schools, clinics and organizations such as the Institute for New Americans.

On the first floor he saw Audrey Crystal speaking with a small, sallow, bespectacled girl. Paris waited. The girl gave him a quick glance and hurried away, rattling a sheaf of papers as she went.

Audrey Crystal turned to him. The redness had left her cheeks and her eyes looked softer than he had remembered. "Have you got everything you need, Captain?" she asked.

"Almost," he said. "What was Mrs. Huntress's attitude to you? Was she grateful, appreciative, perhaps belligerent?"

"She was more confused than anything else. And a bit cautious. You see, not all of these displaced persons understand the mechanics of our charitable organizations. Many are afraid to join. They think that strings are attached. As a matter of fact, many of them, especially Asians, think we're naïve and childish. They've been through some terrible times and they have no comprehension of goodness for goodness' sake. In many of their countries these services are offered only for money. Or for political reasons. They have no volunteer workers like we have. Charity as we know it just doesn't exist there. In India, China, the Middle East, many of these countries' people will literally starve in the gutters. The authorities ignore them completely. There is no help. One doesn't realize that in this country."

"I understand," Paris said. "Now Mrs. Huntress was married. She came from Susz, Poland. Actually, we don't seem to have any more information than that. I'd like to know more about her."

"You might try the Department of State. Or the Immigration and Naturalization Service of the Justice Department. They have joint control over displaced persons' visas. This institute is accredited to both departments of the Government. And another thing. There is a master file kept in Switzerland under the International Refugee Organization. They keep a huge IBM system."

Paris smiled. "Thank you, Mrs. Crystal."

"Not at all." She turned and walked to the large, sweeping staircase and then stopped. She turned back. "By the way, Captain," she said, "when are the visiting hours at the Summerton Hospital?"

Paris grinned. "Any time at all. Trooper Montaigne has a private room."

He went through the heavy iron and glass doors down to the sidewalk. He climbed into his car and sat for a moment, slumped behind the wheel. His eyes went thoughtfully up and down the street. A clean street. And a quiet street. He tried to picture Mrs. Huntress walking down the sidewalk in the cool evening air. Walking carefully and erect. Walking in a plain, cotton, print dress to a dance and an evening with her own people. He turned and looked at the big brownstone. A large American flag flapped lazily back at him in the soft breeze.

He flipped on the ignition and drove up to Beacon Hill and stopped before a tall, stately office building flanked by two grinning concrete lions. He passed down a broad echoing corridor and turned into the offices of the United Community Fund. A stubby blonde in a glaring red-checked blouse looked up and smiled. Paris smiled back. She grinned and pressed a buzzer. Paris grinned back as an office door opened and a tall man in a conservative charcoal-gray suit looked out.

"Wade Paris!" he said. A pair of light-blue eyes twinkled through the black horn-rimmed glasses which Joe Osgood wore high on his nose. "It's been a long time. Come in here and sit down."

Sunlight streamed through the open Venetian blinds and made the office bright and cheerful. Paris said, "I want to know about the Institute for New Americans."

"It's a fine organization, Wade," Osgood said. "Too bad we're unable to support them the way we should. They do great work. But, as you know with funds, there's never enough to go around. Distressing. You get resigned to it after a while. Luckily, the institute has Mrs. Raeder. She underwrites most of their programs."

"I didn't know that," Paris said.

"She likes to keep it anonymous. She's a Boyd. The banking people. Cecelia met Doctor Raeder out on the West Coast about eight years ago. He was a director of a similar refugee institute out there. She was unmarried. They fell in love and got married in California. She persuaded him to come East and take over the directorship of the institute here in Boston. She was a heavy donor and he was a very capable man. An excellent administrator. He's done a huge job with it. People come from all over to study their program. In eight years Raeder has made that place what it is today."

"Do you know Doctor Valerian Zawisza?"

"Where from?"

"Summerton."

"Summerton. Summerton Hospital. Oh, a fine man. One of our key people in that area. A great fund raiser. Hard worker. Very civic minded." Osgood shook his head slowly. "Wade, I'm sorry about the death of that poor woman. But frankly, I can't see where the hospital, the institute or our organization is at fault in anyway."

"Thank you, Joe. You've been a lot of help."

"Next time, give me a ring for lunch."

"I will," Paris said.

He got to his feet, brushed off his hat and walked through the reception room. The blonde in the red-checked blouse swiveled in her chair and winked. "Bye, bye, Captain," she said.

Paris grinned. "So long," he said. He opened the door and turned down the hall.

CHAPTER

18

WADE PARIS sat in his office alone. He leaned back and
frowned at the top of his desk. It was even more littered
than before. There was a report from the laboratories,
and one from the medical examiner. There was a bulky
envelope from the State Police pathologist and a sheaf of
papers describing the activities of his detective lieuten-
ants, his detective sergeants and the two plain-clothes
troopers who were being used for surveillance work. And
now he knew it was time to pull everything together. To
tighten and eliminate the inevitable duplication. To find
a pattern in the hodgepodge wealth of information which
spilled over the green blotter onto the smooth mahogany
of his desk.

Paris reached into the desk drawer, pulled out a pad of
yellow-lined paper and began to write:

Item 1. Dewey Maddox. Age 41. Shot and killed in his
office between 9:00 and 9:20 P.M. Was shot through the
heart and death was almost instantaneous. The gun had
been pushed hard into the flesh. Powder burns on the

clothing. Point of entry larger than exit due to compression of the exploding gases. Bullet had been recovered in the wall in good condition. Striations very sharp. .38 calibre.

He stopped, reached into his pocket and pulled out a crumpled pack of cigarettes. He lit one, and balanced it carefully on the edge of the desk.

Suspects? Many. There were hundreds who hated him and who were in debt to him. Also Mrs. Dewey Maddox. Divorced from Maddox five years ago. Contact had shown she now lived in San Diego. On the night of the murder she had been entertaining a naval officer in her home there. She had shown no interest in coming East for the funeral. A brother, Elmore Maddox from Chicago, had flown in to take care of the arrangements.

Item 2. Mrs. Marie Huntress. Age 46. Died of CO poisoning, carbon monoxide.

Paris reached into the desk drawer and pulled out another long, yellow pencil. He sharpened it. Then he tapped the eraser lightly against the bridge of his nose.

Death caused by inhalation of illuminating gas. Eighty-five per cent saturation in the blood. The blow on the head had been hard enough to cause loss of consciousness and temporary amnesia. No sign of struggle. Nothing under fingernails to show that she had scratched out at her assailant. Negative report on fingerprints. The entire apartment had been wiped clean. Even the bottles of medicine in the medicine chest. She had been dead, when found, approximately four to six hours. That made it approximately between midnight and 2 A.M.

Paris pushed back from the desk and drew thoughtfully on his cigarette. Then he leaned forward and added, *During this time, police had been roaming the Summerton and Lake Islington area.* It had been a busy night, he thought. A very, very busy night.

Item 3. Trooper Frank Montaigne. Age 28. Resting comfortably and taking nourishment. Bullet removed from chest same caliber as that found in the wall of Maddox's office. Same striations. Fired from the same .38 caliber revolver. Unable to enlighten them further as to identity or partial identity of his assailants.

Item 4. Wesley Cagle. Age 26. At home with Parole Officer Tallino until 9:30 that evening, the time when Walter Franz had entered the Cagle residence to take Mrs. Ruth Cagle into custody.

Item 5. Mrs. Ruth Cagle. Age 24. Released in bail of five hundred dollars for carrying a concealed weapon—

There was a knock at his door. He said, "Come in."

A detective stood at the door. "Yes, Sam," Paris said. "What is it?"

"Sorry to bother you, Captain," the detective said. "But I have signed statements from the two women. Their attorney wants to talk with you."

"There's nothing to talk about," Paris said. "Let the assistant D.A. handle it." He knew what it was. The attorney wanted to know if he would accept a lesser plea. The two women had been bogus real-estate buyers. They answered newspaper advertisements of houses for sale. They would call the owner and make an appointment to look at the house, posing as two married sisters. While one engaged the attention of the owner, the other would linger in a bedroom and search quickly for rings, jewelry, money, watches and keepsakes. Any item that could be slipped into a handbag undetected. Usually the man or woman of the house would think they had lost or misplaced the item. Many thefts had gone unreported and they could not hazard a guess as to how many times the crime had been worked. However, there had been a few scattered complaints in the eastern part of the state and from that a pattern had evolved. They began to watch the ads and the detective began to check appointments. The two women had been caught. Neither of them had police records. They were from upper middle-class families, both respectable married women. Doing it for a lark, they said, because they were bored. Now they were full of remorse.

"What do you want to charge them with?" the detective asked.

"How much property did you find on them?"

"Stuff worth about six hundred dollars."

"Grand larceny," Paris said.

The detective looked at him oddly. "They made restitution."

"For the stuff you caught them with," Paris said. "And a few trinkets they had at home. It's grand larceny."

"Yes, Captain," the detective said, and then in a dry voice, "Thanks."

As the door closed quietly behind him, Paris snubbed out his cigarette. He reached into his pocket and pulled out another. Let them call him Old Icewater. But he did not know of any other course. He was thinking of the victims. How many men and women had they stolen from? How many precious mementoes and treasures of great sentimental value had been taken? How many wives had lain awake how many nights afraid to tell husbands of lost diamond rings or watches that had been tenderly presented on some occasion or left as an heirloom of the family? No, this was no lark. And where did you draw the line? When would another pair of women, hearing about the system and knowing of only a light punishment, decide to try it? No, let a judge decide on the punishment.

He turned in his chair and brought his attention back to the yellow pad sitting in his lap.

Item 6. R. A. Annis, D.D.S. age 37, and Mrs. William Appleton, age 62. Mrs. Appleton had been in bad pain with an abscessed tooth, and Dr. Annis had been working hard. Abscessed teeth were touchy things to handle. They had been in the office from 8:30 to 9:30. They heard no shot, no person coming or going. The radio had been on and Dr. Annis had been using a drill.

Murders are touchy things to handle too, thought Paris. Just as touchy as abscessed teeth. He sharpened another pencil and leafed through a report from one of the plainclothes troopers.

Item 7. George "Ducky" Britt, age 55. A small-time thief and general handy man to Dewey Maddox. Maddox had never confided in Britt. Britt was at a wake in Westwood that night. Twenty-five witnesses had testified to his presence at the wake from 7:30 to 11 P.M. He knew of nobody by the name of Marie Huntress. As for suspects to Maddox's murder, a statement from Britt, "Dewey had enough enemies to fill a telephone book. He wasn't the most popular guy in Summerton, you know." He knew nothing of Maddox making a deal to kill a woman at the hospital.

He knew of no records that Maddox kept other than what the police now had. Yes, he knew that Ruth Cagle visited Maddox at his office on occasion.

Item 8. Alfred Weaver. Age 33. He had once gambled heavily with Maddox but had not done so for several years. He owed Maddox no money. He was at home with his wife the night of the murder. Mrs. Alfred (Louise) Weaver corroborated the statement.

Paris found the ash tray under the medical examiner's report, pulled on his cigarette and ground it out.

Item 9. Dr. Valerian Zawisza. Age 52. Dr. Zawisza had a good regard for Mrs. Huntress. He had found she was a refined, educated woman and had tried to make things "easier" for her. He had invited her in for tea several times in his office. She had never been to his home and he had never visited her apartment. But being of the same country of origin he was kindly disposed toward her. She had told him her husband had disappeared on a flight from Poland years ago and that she had given him up for dead. She had told him she met her husband Stanley when they were both students at the University of Poznan. To Dr. Zawisza her story was common enough. Many displaced persons had been caught fleeing the purge. He did not know why she had suddenly become so affluent. She worked no overtime and took no extra jobs. She certainly had not borrowed money from any of the other employees. She was hardly able to converse with them. No money or valuables had been reported stolen from the hospital. No drugs had vanished.

Item 9-A. Mrs. Valerian Zawisza. Age 50. Informants had given information that Mrs. Zawisza was "high-strung and not right in the head." She was "insanely jealous" of her husband. Always "spying" on him. Accused husband of "having affairs with patients and nurses and secretaries." Had once hired a private detective to watch him. When Mrs. Zawisza was interviewed she said she did not know of Mrs. Huntress. Her husband had never mentioned her. The interview was brief and cut short by the witness.

Paris wondered what the detective had found about Doctor Zawisza's private life. A wife's suspicion could easily be exaggerated. But many times there were foundations for her anxieties. *Locate Mrs. Zawisza's private detective,* he wrote. *If possible locate his report on her husband's activities.* Rooting into family difficulties was no fun, he thought. No fun at all.

Item 10. Mrs. Agnes Shepper. Age 69. Landlady at Mrs. Huntress's boarding house. She had never known Mrs. Huntress to have visitors. Rent had always been paid in cash. Mrs. Shepper did admit she was not always in a position to know if Mrs. Huntress had visitors or not.

Item 11. Hugh O'Brien. Age 35. Tenant at boarding house in room next to Mrs. Huntress. He had seen Mrs. Huntress only occasionally. They had never conversed.

Item 11-A. Miss Ethel Hubbard, age 73, Miss Elaine Kantor, age 22 and Mrs. Rose Armbreister, age 40. All employees of the Wardell Tool Company and residing at the Shepper boarding house. Each had seen Mrs. Huntress at one time or another, but had never met her socially or had conversed with her or knew if she had any visitors or acquaintances in Summerton.

Paris stood up and stretched his shoulder muscles. He went over and looked out of the window onto Commonwealth Avenue. It had been a warm day and there was more than the usual number of baby carriages pushing their way through the cool shade in the mall. Here and there a few women were grouped, talking quietly in the roar of traffic passing on either side. Paris watched them absently. There were a few things in the reports that needed more investigating. It just did not seem reasonable that a Polish-American like Doctor Zawisza would meet a Polish refugee and have tea with her in his office, discuss her problems and not mention any of it to his wife. Nor that Mrs. Huntress had come to Boston where she knew not one person and where the Polish population was fairly small. She would have been better off in New York or Chicago or some other Midwestern city. She had asked Doctor Raeder to put her in a place where she would feel more at home. Why did she come to Boston in the first place? Paris scratched his lip thoughtfully. She had certainly become more affluent since the dance of the Polish Cultural Society. She had been living a good deal better than her salary and position had warranted. Had Marie Huntress been a lonely woman? On the exterior, perhaps. But exterior motives didn't count for much. Not in a case like this. Marie Huntress. An educated woman. A teacher in her home country. A woman who knew values and could assimilate facts. Not a woman to make rash decisions on the spur of the moment. Perhaps she had been hunting for someone. Searching through the postwar maze of changing politics: and shifting cultural patterns. Hunting patiently through the complex disorder that lies in the wake of war. Her hunt had led her from Susz, Poland to Summerton, Massachusetts. And now the huntress was dead.

138

He went back to his desk and leafed idly through the papers. Then he sat down and carefully stacked them into neat, exact piles. The facts, he thought. Not speculation. The facts were that two persons were dead and one trooper was recovering from gunshot wounds. The facts lay in the medical reports and the laboratory reports, in the ballistics reports and the reports from his subordinate officers. All of them exacting and accurate. Fact was put down as fact and hearsay was recorded as hearsay. He had to find out more from the State Department. The real name of Marie Huntress. What she did in Poland. What happened to her husband. Why she decided to come to Boston. He had to connect the link between her and Dewey Maddox. But was that the important link? It seemed that Maddox had been only a go-between. He needed to find the connection with the third party at the meeting near the lake. The person who fired the shots at Trooper Montaigne and who later murdered Dewey Maddox. The shadowy third party who was the murderer—or the murderess.

CHAPTER
19

WES CAGLE sat at the kitchen table watching his wife prepare the evening meal. She moved swiftly and precisely,
and never wasted a movement. He didn't bother to ask
what she was making. It smelled good but he wasn't hungry. The tablecloth had a pretty floral design, but the
clear plastic piece which covered it gave forth an acrid
medicinal smell. He had his sleeves rolled up and the plastic stuck to the skin of his elbows. He leaned back and
folded his arms across his chest. His wife's figure looked
good there at the stove. The tight little housedress curved
out sharply from her waist, accentuating the soft snug firm-
ness of her hips. Cagle lowered his eyes and squinted at
the grime in the knuckles of his hand.

"The cops been bothering you much?" he asked.

"No, not much," she said. "How was it at work today?"

"Your brother-in-law treats me like a dog."

"You'll get another job," she said. "Washing cars is not
the worst thing in the world."

The worst thing, he knew, was that his wife was in trouble with the police for carrying a concealed weapon. Plus the fact that she was out on bail that Al Weaver had put up for her.

"They won't indict you," he said.

She turned around. Her face was a deep pink from working over the heat of the stove. She pushed a strand of hair from her forehead and moistened her lips. "They arraigned me, didn't they?"

"They want to keep you around. You co-operate, and they'll nol-pros."

"You've got inside information?"

"No," he said.

"Then don't talk." She turned to the sink and held a glass under the cold water tap. She swallowed once and emptied the rest into the sink. "They're still watching the house," she said. "Every once in a while I see a car come past. It comes by very slowly, and then it speeds up after it's passed."

"Who? Matt Hruska?"

"The state cops."

"They're protecting you."

"Why do you say that?"

"Because," he said, "you're a material witness." He passed his hand over his eyes and sat up carefully in the chair. "They found you running from Dewey Maddox's office."

He waited. The silence was heavy. They had been waiting for it, and when it came it stood like a thick wall between them.

"Now I'll ask you again," he said heavily, "why you went to Dewey's office."

"I don't know."

"You said that the last time I asked you. You didn't know. You did it in a panic."

"Yes."

"Did you go there to kill him?"

"No. I don't know," she said. "Oh, Wes, you can ask me all you want. But I just don't *know*. I wasn't thinking."

"You don't know," he repeated heavily. "You weren't thinking." He stopped and dabbed at the perspiration which had begun to bead his forehead. Then he put his elbows down on the table again and looked blankly at the picture calendar which hung on the wall above his head. A large brown paneled speedboat trailing two small figures on water skis was plunging through the icy blue waters of a high mountain lake. The skiers were waving and their skis threw up white cascades of foam. He turned his eyes away.

"That wasn't the first time you were there, was it?" he said.

She didn't answer. She turned back to the stove, struck a match and lit the burner under the coffee pot.

"I asked you," he said.

She turned and faced him again. "I was never there before in my life, Wes."

"Then why did you go there last night?"

"Because I was afraid for you."

"You could have told me."

"Why? Why should I tell you? When you got that phone call from Dewey that afternoon, did you say anything to *me*? No, you just went out. You didn't say where you were going. I almost went crazy with worry. And then, even when you came *back* you didn't say a word—"

"I went to the State Police."

"I only knew that afterward. But you didn't say a word then. So when the parole officer came I sneaked out to talk to Dewey."

Cagle stood up and went to the sink. He turned on the water and cupped his hands under the flow. Then he rinsed his face quickly and reached for the dry dishtowel.

"Okay," he said. "Just as long as you'd never been there before."

"I was never there before," she said. Because, she thought, her husband knew why women went to Dewey Maddox's office. Many people in Summerton knew. But she had lied to him and she would lie to him again if he asked her. Because she had been to Maddox's office before. If she had told him that the reason for her going was for his sake, to save him from injury or death at the Colony, she knew he would be grateful and understanding. At first, that is. At first he would forgive her magnanimously. Then, little by little, the image of her and Maddox would come back to him. And one day, in a sudden burst of anger, he would blurt out all its ugliness to her. Shouting out at her what a slut she was and worse. Then, of course, the apologies, the contriteness and the forgiveness again. Until another quarrel. No, she had lied to him and she would continue to lie to him emphatically, no matter what he found out. Even if he did become suspicious, as long as she denied it to her last breath, he could never be sure. It was not the first time she had lied to anybody in the case. There was more than

143

Dewey Maddox involved. There was the death of the Huntress woman.

Mrs. Valerian Zawisza sat in the den of their new ranch house on the hill. From the picture window she could see the lights of the hospital below. Her husband sat near the fireplace, his feet propped on the leather ottoman, absorbed in the Boston paper. Built into the oak-paneled walls were the components of his stereophonic sound system. He was using a tape recording this evening, and the moving chords of a heavy symphony throbbed through her head. She sat quietly, twisting the long, bony fingers in her lap, staring at him. He was oblivious of her. He always was, she thought.

She said harshly, "Who was this Marie Huntress?" Her thin, pale face was tense. Her nostrils were dilated. "Who was this woman you never told me about? Somebody you met on your trip to Europe two years ago? Tell me."

He didn't answer. He turned the page of the paper.

"Answer me," she said. "It was at that medical seminar in Vienna."

He sat reading stolidly.

"It was you who brought her over."

He put the paper down and folded it neatly in his lap. "Yes," he said. "I was attracted by her charm and ravishing beauty."

"So she was a ravishing beauty."

"You saw her picture in the paper. A movie star."

"She was a schwakie. You were always soft for Poles."

"I married a Ukrainian," he said.

"But you always loved Polish girls."

"Why not?" he asked equably. He picked up the paper and leafed through the front section absently. "I'm of Polish descent myself."

The music was giving her a splitting headache. She wanted to jump from her chair and rip the wires out of the walls. "You spent a lot of time with that woman in the hospital. I saw you there with her."

"That isn't what you told the police."

"I lied. I lied to save your reputation. I pushed the detective out of here. I didn't want you disgraced by scandal."

"You never saw her with me," he said. "Never. If you did, you'd have had her fired. Every nurse, secretary and technician under forty and halfway decent looking you've had me fire. If you knew of this irresistible, delectable creature, why didn't you demand I fire her?"

Her thin hands gripped the arms of the chair. "So she's not beautiful. How do I know that in your warped, diseased mind you didn't find her attractive?"

He didn't answer her. He leaned his head against the back of the chair and closed his eyes.

She picked up the ginger-ale glass on the table beside her and sipped. "Valerian, where were you on the night she was killed?"

"Where were you, Gerda?" he asked.

"In my bedroom," she said. "I took a sleeping pill. I fell asleep watching television. You wouldn't know. You never come to my room any more."

"Please, Gerda," he said. "I'm sick of this harping."

"You run around with other women," she said. "Me, you allow no pleasures. Nothing. Not even a little wine.

You don't allow me to bet on the horses any more. I suppose you're glad Maddox is dead."

He opened his eyes and stared blankly at the ceiling. "Yes," he said. "I'm glad. He was no good. Both of you cost me a lot of money."

"You're in love with money. Just because I did a little harmless gambling—"

"Stop it," he said. "Dewey Maddox was coming here to the house. Do you realize the gossip it would have caused if people found out?"

"He's dead now. He can't talk." She put her glass down, making a wet circle on the waxed surface of the table. "Why do you hate me so much, Valerian?"

"I've never hated you, Gerda. I feel sorry for you."

"Why do you feel sorry for me?"

"Because you're an alcoholic and you're a neurotically jealous woman."

"You mean I'm insane."

"I said neurotic."

"You mean psychotic."

"I said what I meant. Neurotic."

"You keep thinking about that one time that I tried to kill you with the bread knife."

"And the receptionist at the hospital," he said.

"A strumpet," she said. "You've got friends. You hushed it all up. You fixed it up with Matt Hruska. He's a Polack too."

"He knew it would be bad for the hospital and the town." He turned his head and looked at her. "Why don't you divorce me, Gerda?"

"Where would I go?"

"You must have friends."

"I have nobody."

"You have relatives."

"I can't stand them. They're cheap, ignorant people. Why should I divorce you? I'm Mrs. Valerian Zawisza. I'm one of the most important people in Summerton. Why should I give it up? Besides, now since your schwakie is dead, you'll pay a little more attention to me. Or have you another one in the hospital?"

"Dozens," he said. "I have a different one every hour."

"I know you have. I will find them out one by one. I'll make them so miserable they'll leave."

"You try that," he said, "and I'll leave orders not to allow you to enter the hospital."

"You see how much you despise me," she said.

"As a matter of fact, Gerda, I do."

She picked up the glass of ginger ale and threw it at him. He saw it coming and ducked his head in time. The glass smashed against the oak paneling and the liquid spread darkly down the wall onto the carpet.

CHAPTER

20

It had been a hot day for early June. Audrey Crystal had eaten a hurried meal in the small restaurant on Copley Square where she dined every Wednesday evening and had returned to the Institute. She didn't mind these late nights. They kept her busy. There was usually extra work to attend to if Dr. Raeder had been away all day. Some administrative problems had come up while he was gone. They would work until nine-thirty or ten o'clock and then he would see her home, leaving her at her apartment with a brisk, curt thank you and good night. One thing about Dr. Raeder. He was always formal and correct with his employees. Overly so, sometimes.

She was sitting with him in the large office on the second floor. The French windows were open but there was not much breeze and it was quite warm in the room.

Dr. Raeder was at his desk. His white shirt was starched and crisp. His hair was freshly barbered and he looked very cool. When she brought some folders to his desk she could smell the sharp aroma of an expensive men's cologne.

"Sit down a moment, Mrs. Crystal," he said to her. He smiled briefly. "I am always sorry to keep you here so late."

"I don't mind at all," she said. "What would I do otherwise?"

"You could be out with a nice young man."

"No. I'd be sitting alone in my apartment."

"I find that difficult to believe, Mrs. Crystal. Have you ever thought of remarrying?"

"Oh, yes. I would like to very much, but so far I haven't found anybody I want."

"There is the policeman."

"What policeman?"

"The captain of the State Police."

"Captain Paris?" She laughed and pushed a wisp of hair from her forehead. "He's a little too old for me. Besides, he's too wrapped up in his work to notice me."

"You make me feel ancient, Mrs. Crystal. Captain Paris must be in his late thirties." He smiled. "A very mature age," he said.

"I hardly know him, Doctor."

"The point is to get to know him. That should not be too difficult. You are a very attractive girl."

"Thank you," she said. She felt a warmth in her cheeks and wondered if it showed. Dr. Raeder didn't seem to notice. She lowered her eyes and said, "But I don't want to appear too obvious."

"No, that would not do. He is a deceptively clever man. You must think a bit." He stretched back in the chair and folded his hands behind his head. "Try to find something in common."

"What?"

"Well, how did you first meet him? What initiated his coming here?"

"Mrs. Huntress—the woman who died in Summerton."

"Precisely." He smiled and sat up in the chair. He opened the drawer and found his cigarette case. "Discuss the case with him. After all, you have some knowledge of it. You've met the woman. He hasn't. That is how those things start."

"I'm afraid not," she said. "I know nothing more about the case. Besides he is not for me and I am not for him. As a matter of fact he asked me to visit the trooper who was shot."

"Oh," Raeder said. "And why not do it?"

"That's right," she said. "Why not?"

"The papers say he is recovering from his wounds. I am sure he is a fine young man." He pushed the cigarette case toward her. She shook her head. He picked one out, snapped his lighter, and stared thoughtfully through the open French windows to the balcony outside. A large electric fan stood motionless on a black, metal stand just inside the windows. He placed his cigarette on the hollowed lip of the ash tray. "It is sad about Mrs. Huntress," he said. "She struggled so hard to arrive at a haven only to die a few weeks after she had finally found it. I had quite a chat with her at the Polish Cultural Society dance." He shook his head moodily. "I came from Mecklenburg, which is in Northern Germany. She came from Susz, Poland, which is not so far from Danzig. When I was young I went to Danzig

150

quite a number of times when it was a free city under the League of Nations mandate. There was an excursion boat that sailed there in the summer. She had been there too. Perhaps we had once bumped into one another on the streets or sat at adjoining tables in some cafe, never knowing that our paths would cross so many years later here in the United States."

"You must have had much to talk about, Doctor."

"Oh, yes. Do you know what most people talk about at those dances?" he asked. She shook her head. "Everyone talks about how good it was in the old days. How wonderful it was in the homeland. Poland was a poor country, but one forgets the hard parts. I remember a visit to Poland, and I think only of the rich, black earth and the large, brown potatoes that came from it." He smiled and drew slowly on his cigarette. "One forgets the filthy, mud-rutted streets of the villages, the tiny, log huts with their cramped outhouses and the unwashed people in their muddy boots. It is odd how the mind changes. How the unpleasantness and the hardness of life are so easily forgotten. Mrs. Huntress spoke of the hot summers and the bitter cold winters. But she spoke of them with zest and yearning."

"Do you ever yearn for Germany, Doctor?"

"Oh, yes. What is more dear to one's heart than the place of his youth? But it is more pleasant and luxurious here. I know I would return only as a visitor." He smiled. "Had I stayed there all my life I probably would not have risen as high in stature as I am now."

"Or as low as Mrs. Huntress," she said. "She was a teacher in Poland. Here she was a scrubwoman."

"Yes, that was unfortunate. Many displaced people have

lost stature. To hear them talk they were at least the mayor of the village, or a baron, a graf, freiherr, a boyar or gospodin. But not Mrs. Huntress. She was a well educated person. It is very sad."

Audrey Crystal could see a softness in his eyes that she had never noticed before, and suddenly she knew she was blushing again. She fumbled for the right words and then finally asked, "I don't understand why she was killed."

"It is mystifying and terrifying to me too. She was nobody here. She knew nobody. She seemed to have nothing that anyone might want. This is a strange country of great charity and warmth and generosity on one hand and appalling brutality on the other. Who knows what strange motive there was. Perhaps it was a madman."

She looked down at her hands, and then as the silence grew between them, said, "I'm afraid I took you away from your work."

"Yes, I guess we have wandered a bit." He stretched his neck. "You have the file on the Albanian League?"

"Here on your desk."

"Yes, thank you, Mrs. Crystal." He opened the folder and carefully leafed through the thick sheaf of papers. Then he pushed back from the desk. "Do you find it warm here?"

"It is warm for this time of year," she said. "But I don't mind so much."

"I think we will put in an air-conditioning unit next year. Meanwhile I had better put on the fan and circulate some of the air."

He got up from the desk, walked over to the windows and switched on the fan. He came back and sat down. She pulled her chair closer and opened her stenographic notebook. The fan hummed steadily. The air ruffled through the room, stirring the papers.

"Now," he said, "this month we have four meetings in the big hall—"

Suddenly she saw a flash of fire from the open balcony, and then a violent explosion.

He grabbed her by the shoulder. "Down!" he shouted. "Quickly!"

She slid out of her chair and down to the floor behind the big desk. He came down beside her on his knees. She turned toward him, her heart fluttering with fright.

"Somebody fired a shot at us," he said hoarsely, urgently. "I will move to the right to draw their attention. When I do, you crawl out to the door, run down and telephone the police. Do you know the number?"

She took a deep breath. "Devonshire 1212."

He crawled to his right and shouted, "Who is there?"

The steady hum of the electric fan filled the room. There was no sound from the balcony. She crawled on her hands and knees away from the window across the polished, wooden floor toward the door.

"Now," he whispered back to her.

She got up in a crouching position and ran for the door. No sound. She clattered down the wide, arching staircase to the first floor. There was a night light over the reception desk and underneath that she saw the telephone. She picked up the receiver and dialed the number. When the police dispatcher answered she slowly told him her name and address. Almost too slowly, for the voice of the dispatcher suddenly crackled over the line.

"What's the problem, Miss?"

"There's been a shooting," she said, and then suddenly dropping the receiver back on the cradle, she pushed her balled fists against her mouth. She squeezed them hard against her lips, pushing back the scream which grew in her throat. She stood frozen for a moment and then slowly relaxed. She brought her arms down to her sides, took a deep breath, and then carefully walked to the foot of the staircase.

"Doctor Raeder," she called. "Are you all right?"

"I am fine," he answered and then she could see him coming to the top of the stairs. He seemed very pale to her as he walked carefully down the steps. He said, "How are you, Mrs. Crystal?"

She rubbed her knee and smiled weakly. "All right, except I have a run in my stocking."

"Cigarette?"

"Yes, thank you." She took the cigarette with a trembling hand and waited as he lit it. "I've a hard knot inside me," she said. "What happened?"

"I think somebody climbed up the fire escape to the balcony and tried to shoot one of us. The shot went wild. He must have gone down the fire escape and got away. Is the front door locked?"

"Yes."

"The back?"

"It was when I went out earlier. Should I check it?"

"No, you stay here with me. We will wait for the police."

She waited. He stood there beside her smoking, his face shadowed in the dimly lit foyer. She tried to listen for the sound of police sirens. There were none. Just the steady hum of traffic and the occasional sound of a car horn.

Then the bell rang and there was a hammering on the door.

Dr. Raeder went over and parted the curtains at the side glass, then he unlocked the door. Two Boston policemen stood there in their dark blue uniforms. In front, double parked beside the cars which lined the curb, sat two police cars, their roof lights flashing.

"You call about the shooting?" one of the policemen asked.

"I did," Audrey Crystal said, moving to the door. She saw the revolver in his hand by his side, the muzzle pointing downward.

"Anybody hurt?"

"No, they missed."

"Good. Where did the shot come from?"

"Outside in back," she said. And then she added almost hysterically, "Where were the sirens?"

"The what?" he said, coming inside.

"The sirens on the police car."

"Oh," the policeman said and then he grinned. "No, lady. There's no reason to advertise our coming, is there? Why frighten the criminal away? Right?"

She smiled wanly. "Right."

"You okay?" he asked.

"Yes."

There was a pounding from the rear of the building.

The policeman turned and said to her, "There are some officers out back. Would you show me how to let them in?"

"I will show you," Dr. Raeder said. "This way, please."

Audrey Crystal stood at the open door, looking past the policeman. As she watched, a small crowd began to gather on the sidewalk. She looked up and saw the dark outlines of people in the apartment house across the street, framed against their lighted windows, leaning out to see what the disturbance was. She wanted to laugh, because it suddenly seemed as if she were standing in the middle of a large and garish Hollywood motion-picture set. Then she remembered how real the shot had been and how loud the explosion. She carefully walked to the chair behind the reception desk.

"Are you all right, Miss?" the policeman asked.

"Yes, I think so," she said. She sat down and slumped back in the chair. "Yes," she said slowly. "I'm fine, thank you very much."

Dr. Raeder took the policeman through the corridor to the rear of the house. The door was fireproof and made of steel. Raeder pulled back the bolt and the policeman swung the door open. Outside was another policeman. He looked at the two and then holstered his revolver. "Nothing out here, Denny," he said.

The first policeman turned to Raeder and asked, "What's your name, mister?"

"Doctor Fritz Raeder. I am director of the Institute."

"Where did the shot come from, Doctor?"

"I will show you," Raeder said. He stepped out through the open door to the back and turned right to the fire escape which rose up along the side of the building. Two plain-clothes men were standing underneath it, focusing their flashlights up to the second-floor balcony.

One turned to the policeman and said, "Who's this, Denny?"

"Doctor Raeder, the director."

"Okay," the plain-clothes man said. He pointed the beam from his flashlight up toward the balcony again. "Denny, give me a hand, will you?"

The policeman and the other detective locked their hands together and made a place for his foot. Then they boosted him up. He grabbed the end of the fire escape ladder and canted it downward. Then he climbed up the ladder to the projecting step near the balcony. He swung his flashlight around and then lifted himself up to the floor of the balcony.

"Got it," he called down.

Dr. Raeder, peering up through the darkness, saw the detective's shadow bend downward. He turned to the other plain-clothes man. "He has got what?"

"A gun," the man said. "Let's go inside."

CHAPTER
21

THE plain-clothes man's name was Sullivan. He and Dr. Raeder stood alone in the large, second-floor office. The French doors to the balcony were still open. A small breeze had begun to move past the curtains into the room. Sullivan was a stocky, young red-faced man. He was holding the revolver by the checkered butt between his thumb and forefinger. He studied it thoughtfully for a moment and then dropped it into a box.

Dr. Raeder asked him, "Will you check it for fingerprints?"

"Sure," Sullivan said. "Ballistics will. I've been in the business for ten years and I've never yet found a decent fingerprint on a gun." He walked over to the far wall and cocked his head back and looked up at the bullet hole circled high on the pale green wall beyond the desk. "Doctor Raeder, you're lucky. Whoever it was, was a lousy shot, or too excited and nervous. Now, tell me everything as it happened."

Raeder told him—from the time that he and Audrey

Crystal had sat down to the time they'd seen the flash and heard the shot. He told how Mrs. Crystal had rushed down to phone the police and how they'd waited downstairs until the squad cars had appeared. Sullivan made notes. Then he said, "You were both sitting behind the desk here?"

"Yes, sir."

"Did you see anything from the balcony?"

"No, I was not looking."

"After the shot?"

"Nothing."

"And you were sitting side by side?"

"We were checking some papers," said Raeder.

"Then the shot could have been for Mrs. Crystal instead of for you?"

Raeder suddenly jerked his head up and looked at him. "Why, yes. I never thought of that."

"When you left her and turned on the fan you saw nothing on the balcony?"

"No, sir. And I was looking straight at it. The balcony was quite empty. Perhaps the gunman was crouching down."

"Do you have any enemies, Doctor Raeder?"

"I believe not. We are engaged in charitable and rehabilitation work here. I cannot understand why anyone would want to harm me."

"No personal enemies, Doctor?"

"None that I know of."

"How long have you been in this country?"

"Thirteen years."

"You had trouble a few days ago, didn't you?"

"Trouble? You mean the death of Mrs. Huntress? Yes, but that did not happen here."

"I know. In Summerton. Was she a member of any of the organizations here?"

"No, she was a member of nothing."

"Who from the State Police talked to you?"

"Captain Paris."

"The Chief of Detectives?"

"Yes. He came himself."

Sullivan scratched his jaw and walked slowly to the center of the large room. "Thank you, Doctor. Would you have Mrs. Crystal come in now?"

Captain Wade Paris sat in the office of the Bureau of Criminal Investigation at Boston Police Headquarters in the gray stone building on Berkeley Street. The BCI head was Captain O'Rourke, a lean middle-aged, partially bald man with a black mustache which bushed out darkly above his thin mouth. He bowed his head and talked quietly with Paris. A trooper had been shot and was fighting for his life following the operation that had removed the .38 slug from his chest. Then a small-town racketeer, Dewey Maddox, had been killed. Now either a Mrs. Audrey Crystal or a Dr. Fritz Raeder had been shot at, and all with the same gun.

"At least we have the gun," O'Rourke said. He eyed the wire mesh mail basket perched on the corner of his desk. He reached over and pulled out a folded paper. He snapped it open and spread it on the desk. "According to the Ballistics Report it was a Colt Cobra, .38 special with a four-inch barrel and a square-checkered walnut butt. No detectable fingerprints, two cartridges left in the cylinder. The cartridges were .38 Winchester Center Fire, Colt New Police. Common enough. Purchasable almost anywhere." He smoothed the paper out and read on. They had not been able to trace the gun. According to the serial number, the factory had shipped it out to a wholesaler in Racine, Wisconsin, in 1957. The entire shipment had been stolen a month later. The gun could have gone anywhere after that.

"Funny that the gun would be dropped on the fire escape," Paris said.

"Yeah," said O'Rourke. "Maybe the guy slipped and fell as he ran down. It could have slipped out of his hand and he didn't want to take the chance of going back for it."

"Maybe," Paris said. "What do you think, Danny?"

"How about that Mrs. Cagle?"

"No. We had her under surveillance."

"Who is this Mrs. Audrey Crystal?"

"Lives on Marlboro Street," Paris said. He stood up and cocked his arms by his sides. Then he pushed his elbows backward and stretched the muscles below his shoulders. "Family came from Pittsfield. Graduated from Simmons College. A social worker. Married an Air Force jet pilot."

"Did he go down?"

"No, not in the way you mean." Paris frowned and sat down. "Met another girl and fell in love. Audrey Crystal gave him his divorce soon afterward."

"Any kids?"

"No."

"Any boy friends?"

"Can't find any." Paris pulled at his ear. "What do you know about Raeder?"

"He married Cecelia Boyd," O'Rourke said. "Cecelia Boyd inherited five million bucks about nineteen years ago when she became twenty-one. She never married. Got interested in charity work. The Institute was her pet. About eight years ago she went out West to a convention in Los Angeles. She met Raeder who was at that time the head of some small agency out there. She wanted him to come East and head up the Institute for New Americans. And she made it worth his while to do it. So he came to Boston. A year later they were married. He still heads the Institute."

Paris frowned. "I bet he doesn't do it for eating money," he said.

"No, but it's his work and he likes it."

Someone knocked on the door. Paris got to his feet and pulled it open. A uniformed policeman came in. He put his hands down on the desk, leaned over and whispered in O'Rourke's ear. Then he went out.

O'Rourke stood up. "We've got company. Mrs. Raeder is outside."

"I'll go," Paris said.

"No, stay, Wade. If she's going to chew me out, I'm going to need some support. She's got more connections than I have."

He went outside and Paris stood alone for a moment. He looked at his watch and then fumbled through his pockets for a cigarette. He found one and put it in his mouth. Then he stuffed it back in the package. Mrs. Raeder might

162

not like cigarette smoke and now was no time to find out whether she did or she didn't.

A moment later, O'Rourke came back with a woman. She was tall and angular with high cheekbones, a long sharp nose and chin. She was plainly dressed in a plain brown suit. She wore no make-up and her brown hair was streaked with gray. Her legs were thin and she wore brown, low-heeled shoes.

She looked at Paris.

"This is Captain Wade Paris," O'Rourke said. "Chief of Detectives, State Police. Captain, Mrs. Fritz Raeder."

"How do you do," she said. "Why don't we sit down?"

O'Rourke drew up a chair for her. She sat down and carefully crossed her ankles. Then she turned to O'Rourke. "Now tell me what is being done about my husband's assailant."

"Ma'am," O'Rourke said, "it takes time."

"An attempt was made on his life. What's being done about it?"

"Everything we can," O'Rourke said.

"Words," she said, and Paris thought he heard her sniff ever so slightly. "Nothing but words. I want specifics."

"We have a lot of people to check out," O'Rourke said. "It's police business."

"A gun was found. What about it?"

"We're checking it out, ma'am," O'Rourke said.

"I don't want to have to go upstairs to the Police Commissioner," she said. "My husband was shot at and I want to know what's being done about it."

"I've told you everything we can," O'Rourke said gently. "You can go to the commissioner if you want. But he hasn't got anything more than I have."

She turned impatiently to Paris. "Are the State Police interested in this?"

"Part of it," Paris said.

"What part?"

"The gun that was used against your husband was also involved in the shooting of one of our troopers."

Mrs. Raeder lifted an eyebrow.

"It was also used in the murder of a man in Summerton," Paris said.

"Dewey Maddox?" she asked.

"Yes. You know him?"

"Only by name. It was in the papers."

"We spoke to your husband," O'Rourke said. "He says he has no enemies. Would you know of anyone who wanted to harm him?"

"No. He has no enemies. Why should he have enemies?" she asked impatiently.

"It's always possible that the shot was meant for Mrs. Crystal."

"I have thought of that," she said grudgingly.

"Did you know Marie Huntress?" Paris asked.

"No. I heard she had come from the Institute but I had never met her."

"Did you ever know a Wesley Cagle or a Ruth Cagle?" Paris asked. He stood up and leaned with one hand against the corner of O'Rourke's desk.

"I never heard of them. Who are they?"

"They're connected with another case," Paris said. "Mrs. Raeder, where were you last night?"

164

"Why?"

"Just for the record, Mrs. Raeder."

"I see. Even I'm suspect. Is that it?"

"No, ma'am. We just try to eliminate every possibility we can."

"I was at a meeting of the United Community Fund at their offices on Beacon Street. I was there from seven until ten."

"Is there anybody who could vouch for your presence the entire time?"

"Yes. Mr. Bridges. Mrs. Warren. Mrs. Peabody."

"Was Mr. Osgood there?"

"Joe Osgood? Yes. Of course, I did wander around a bit. But I did leave with Mrs. Warren. You may call her."

She gave Paris the telephone number. He jotted it down. She looked at him with a pinched face.

"How did your husband come to this country?" O'Rourke asked.

"He entered under the German quota."

"As a refugee?" Paris asked.

"As a displaced person and political refugee. He was both anti-Nazi and anti-Communist."

O'Rourke leaned back in his chair. "He was an officer in the German Army of World War II."

"Against his will. He had been a reservist. He had no choice. All able-bodied Germans, anti-Nazi or not, were called up to the Army."

"Oh?" said Paris. He slumped into his chair and watched a fly buzzing futilely against the window pane.

"So were a number of Belgians, Dutch, and Danes," she said.

"Tell me, Mrs. Raeder," O'Rourke said, "what do you think of Mrs. Crystal?"

Mrs. Raeder pinched her thin lips together and lifted a gloved hand to her mouth. She coughed discreetly and then cleared her throat. "Mrs. Crystal is a very efficient assistant."

"Do you know anything else about her?"

"She's very pretty. You must know that, of course."

"Anything else?"

"Yes," Mrs. Raeder said. "It's very obvious that she's infatuated with my husband."

"Does it bother you, ma'am?" O'Rourke asked.

"No. Dr. Raeder is a handsome, distinguished man. Many other women have been infatuated with him. It has done them no good. It will do Mrs. Crystal no good."

"So there's no friction between you and Mrs. Crystal?"

"Hardly. She's an employee. I can have her discharged at any time if I wished. And if somebody is trying to kill her and her presence is a danger to my husband, I will do just that." She sat back in her chair and smiled wanly. "Are you through with the questioning?"

"Yes," O'Rourke said. He glanced at Paris. "Captain?"

"Yes. Thank you, Mrs. Raeder."

"Now we're back to where we started," Mrs. Raeder said. "What exactly have you done on this case, Captain?"

"We questioned a lot of people," O'Rourke said. "Neighbors, people in the vicinity, anyone else we could find. We have established the time of the shooting. Now we're checking every remote aspect—every lead. If you have any further information—"

Mrs. Raeder got up stiffly and turned toward Paris.

"I've told you all I know," she said. "All I can add is that I expect diligence and swift action."

Both men rose to their feet. "Yes, ma'am," O'Rourke said. He smiled and offered his hand. Mrs. Raeder looked blankly at him for a moment. Then she turned and left the office without a word.

O'Rourke sat down heavily. He ran the back of his hand across his forehead and frowned down at the desktop. "You know something funny?" he said. "I don't blame her. She's been waiting for something to happen and nothing has. Not a damn thing."

"I've been waiting too," Paris said. "What about Dewey Maddox, Danny? Did he have any Boston connections?"

"No."

"He must have laid off some of his bigger gambling plays around here somewhere."

"He did," O'Rourke said. "But our stoolies tell us he always made good. Never had any trouble in Boston. Nobody here wanted to move in on him. Too small. Couldn't be bothered. He had a safety-deposit box in the Boston bank—about two thousand dollars cash. Some common stocks worth about three thousand dollars. Not much," O'Rourke said.

Paris stuck his hands into his hip pockets and looked puzzled. "No bank account? The one in Summerton had less than a thousand dollars. He must have had more than that."

O'Rourke sighed. "He was bleeding a lot of people. He must have been a pretty big spender."

"Something bothers me. Raeder lives in Winchester and Mrs. Crystal here in Boston. Up until now all the action was in Summerton, south of Boston. It breaks the pattern."

"Come on out and I'll buy you some lunch," O'Rourke said.

"Thanks, Danny, but there's work to do."

"You going to check on Mrs. Raeder?"

Paris grinned. "Aren't you?"

CHAPTER

22

A WEEK went by. The medical, ballistic and laboratory reports on Dewey Maddox and Marie Huntress were now complete. As the days went by, more and more of Wade Paris' time was taken up by the many other cases which kept coming into his office. A professor had stolen some money and had been picked up trying to get out of the state. The college did not want the man prosecuted for they wanted no publicity. An employee at a state mental hospital had committed an assault on a young female patient. There was an investigation of smuggling by a civilian employee at a penal institution. A rash of bad checks had broken out in the southwestern part of the state. There was a suicide in Leominster which had to be investigated. A judge had been accepting bribes in land damage cases and his detectives had finished collecting the evidence. A man had spent five hours in a Boston saloon, returned home, picked up an ax and killed his wife. There were cases of narcotics and a nursing-home death which had been caused by criminal neglect. There had been some trouble in the Port Authority and a suspected fraud by persons collecting from the Department of Public Welfare. Some valuable equipment had been stolen from the Department of Public Works.

Paris was short of help. The uniformed branch was short too, but he was able to draw upon them for troopers in plain clothes. When he did that, the traffic patrols always suffered. But they had to do the best with what they had.

One of his queries from the State Department had come in. Marie Huntress had come through the Marienfelde Refugee Center in West Berlin. Her home had been Susz, Poland, and her real name was not Huntress. It had been Marie Lowczyna.

Now he was beginning to move faster. The net was tightening; his men were working and checking every detail. There was nobody by the name of Lowczyna in the Polish Cultural Society or in the Greater Boston area. But he knew he was on the right track.

That week, accompanied by Lieutenant Joe McKenney, he drove out to the Summerton Hospital to visit Trooper Frank Montaigne. Montaigne was seated in a cushion lounge chair on a screened-in porch at the rear of the hospital. From where he sat, he could look directly to the top of the hill and see the ranch house of Dr. Valerian Zawisza.

The trooper had lost weight and his cheeks were pale.

"How do you feel?" Paris asked.

"Good, sir," Montaigne said. "The doctor tells me I'm going home at the end of the week."

"That's great," Paris said. He pulled up a canvas chair and sat down. "Now, Frank, I know we've been over this before. Maybe you've refreshed your memory since the night of the shooting." He searched through his pockets and pulled out a pack of cigarettes. "Sometimes you remember something a long while after it happens. It comes back to you. Some little detail which could help wrap up the case."

"I'll try."

Paris tilted back in the small chair and held a match to his cigarette. "Now we'll go back to when you were walking along the road. You saw nobody until the car came?"

"That's right, sir."

"Is it at all possible that someone was tracking you along the road on foot?"

"No, I don't think so. It was a very still night. I could have heard a rabbit in there."

"How about an expert tracker? Somebody in sneakers, or rubber-soled shoes?"

"Well," Montaigne said doubtfully, "I don't know, Captain. My ears are pretty sharp."

"The point is this. Maddox drove up to you in a car. You saw nobody else with him. As far as you were concerned he was alone."

"Yes, sir."

"When did the other person appear?"

"While I was talking to Maddox."

"Then the only other thing could have been that the second person had been ducked down in the car the whole time," Paris said. "Had Maddox left the car door open?"

"Yes, sir."

"Then they could have been together?"

"Yes, sir."

171

"Now this person was dressed in black. It was dark. You said he was of medium height and of medium build. Can you recall the general shape?"

Montaigne shifted slightly against the arm of the lounge chair. "He was wearing a crewneck sweater with a jacket over it. He had a black felt hat and that black stocking over his face. Gloves, I think. It was dark, Captain."

"How about the shoulders? Narrow? Wide?"

"I'm sorry, Captain."

"Hips?"

"I couldn't tell you, Captain."

"This person," Paris said. "He didn't say a word?"

"No, sir."

"And while you were talking, he suddenly took out a revolver and shot you. Why? Perhaps he was getting suspicious of the questioning. Perhaps he didn't like to be merely the third party. So he pushed the panic button."

"Yes, sir. That could be it, Captain."

"Now then, the reason for his silence. No comment to you. No comment to Maddox. Nothing. Why? We've been giving it some thought. Frank, you'd recognize a foreign accent, wouldn't you?"

"Yes, sir."

"And a Boston accent, too, wouldn't you?"

"Yes, sir."

"And one more thing," Paris said. "You'd recognize a woman's voice, wouldn't you?"

Montaigne smiled. "I sure would, sir."

"Do you think it could have been a woman, Frank?"

Montaigne thought for a moment. "Yes, sir. It might

have been. I've been thinking about that possibility for some time, sir."

"Thanks," Paris said. He stood up. "Take care of yourself, kid." He patted the boy on the shoulder and started out the door with McKenney.

"Captain," Montaigne called.

Paris turned. Montaigne said, "There was a girl out here to see me. She brought me a book. She said her name was Audrey Crystal."

"When was this?"

"Yesterday. She said you asked her to visit me."

"How did you two get along?"

Montaigne hesitated. "Captain—"

Paris said, "She wasn't that bad, was she?"

"I've never met a girl like her, Captain. I mean—well, when I get out of here—that is, if she'll go out with me—"

"That was the general idea."

"There's nothing wrong about it, is there? She asked a lot of questions about the case."

"What did you tell her?"

"What could I? I know so little about it."

"That's all right," Paris said. "Just a woman's natural curiosity. Did she say anything about visiting you again?"

Montaigne smiled. "No, not really. But she said she was going to visit my little girl. I think she might."

"What makes you think so?"

"Well, nothing really. But I think she will." Montaigne looked up. "I appreciate your telling her about me, Captain. You know, since my wife died—"

"Yeah," Paris said. "I'm a hell of a matchmaker."

He turned and walked down the hall with McKenney. McKenney looked at him unblinkingly.

"Shut up," Paris said.

McKenney smiled. "I didn't say a word, Captain," he said.

CHAPTER

23

WADE PARIS stood beside the car for a moment, his arms crossed, staring across the hospital parking lot. He frowned and looked down at the fine black cinders by his feet. He scuffed at them with the toe of his shoe and turned to McKenney.

"Do you want to drive?" he asked.

McKenney nodded and climbed behind the wheel. "Where to?" he said.

"I'd like to pay a call on Doctor Raeder."

McKenney said, "Okay," and turned on the ignition. He pulled the car out onto the highway and they drove back into Boston.

The receptionist at the Institute for New Americans looked up from a magazine and smiled. She said that Dr. Raeder was not in. But Mrs. Crystal was. She phoned upstairs. Mrs. Crystal would see them.

They walked up the wide staircase. Audrey Crystal was waiting for them at the top.

"I'm sorry Doctor Raeder isn't in today," she said. "He's

at an important meeting." She smiled. "More fund raising. It never stops."

They walked into the high-ceilinged room. Paris saw that the French windows were closed and curtained. "How are the Raeders?" he asked.

Audrey Crystal smiled. "They're fine," she said.

Paris looked at the French windows and then walked over to them. There was a key in the lock. He turned it and opened the doors. He walked out onto the balcony and looked down at the fire ladder. Across the yard he could see the backs of the buildings on Marlboro Street. He stepped to the edge of the balcony and squinted back into the room. He squatted on his heels and took a fix with his eye. When he came back in he looked up at the big fan standing by the doors.

"It looks like a powerful fan," Paris said.

"Yes," she said. "Doctor Raeder hopes, someday, to put in an air conditioner. But we need money for so many other things. He never thinks of his personal comfort."

"I understand," Paris said. He looked back at the fan and then pulled the string which was attached to a switch near the motor. The fan revolved slowly for a moment and then began turning rapidly. It gave off a low humming sound which filled the room.

"Not too noisy, is it?" Paris said. He switched off the motor. The fan turned for a few moments and then came to a stop. "You would think that if somebody wanted to shoot Doctor Raeder that night, he would have had a much easier target when Raeder came over here to turn on the fan."

176

"Oh," she said, and her hand moved toward the soft white lace collar at her throat. "You mean the shot was meant for me?"

Paris didn't answer. He moved to the center of the room and looked back at the French windows. "You told us you never knew Dewey Maddox?"

"No, I never heard of him before."

"How about George Britt? His nickname was Ducky."

"No," she said. "Should I know him?"

"He worked for Dewey Maddox in Summerton," Paris said. He looked at her and noticed that she was pulling gently on the small gold-colored bracelet she was wearing on her wrist. "I understand you went to visit Trooper Frank Montaigne."

"Yes, I did," she said. "Were you surprised?"

"Yes, I was," he said.

She took a quick glance at McKenney, who sat smoking a cigarette quietly by the door. "You intrigued me," she said. "After you had gone I began to think of Frank Montaigne and his little girl. I began thinking about them a lot." She smiled. "You know what the best thing to do is when you're thinking a lot about something?"

Paris smiled back. "Go and see whatever you're thinking about?"

"Yes."

"Are you glad you did?"

"I am, very much. It cleared up a lot of feelings for me. That may surprise you, but it really did." She crossed her arms and leaned back against the desk. "I've been heading the wrong way down a one-way street for a long time. I think I've known it all along. But seeing your trooper up there in the hospital made it very real for me." She turned and looked at Paris. "I hope I'm not embarrassing you."

"Of course not," he said. "Did you visit his daughter?"

"Captain, I'd like you to know that your trooper has one of the sweetest, most huggable little girls I've ever known."

Paris grinned. "I'm glad to hear it."

She turned away and stepped behind her desk. "You're surprised at my actions, aren't you? But you did ask me to see him."

"I did," said Paris. He paused for a moment and then said, "But I thought you were in love with somebody else."

"Doctor Raeder?"

"Yes."

"Did it show that much?"

"It showed. How long had you felt that way?"

"About two years. I think you're the first one who ever noticed it," she said. She stopped and ran her finger along the smooth edge of the desk. "Or mentioned it to me," she added.

"Not Doctor Raeder?"

"Definitely not. He doesn't know I exist except as a worker here."

"Don't underestimate him," Paris said. "I think he knew. I think Mrs. Raeder knew also."

"I was never much in her presence. Yes, I guess it's possible she knew. Women can usually tell about those things."

"Especially a man's wife," Paris said.

178

"If she's astute."

"Don't you think Mrs. Raeder is astute?"

"In every respect. Except when it comes to her husband."

"Woman's intuition?" he said.

Audrey Crystal looked away. She moved to her chair and sat down. "Yes," she said.

"I see. Has she ever discussed her husband with you?"

"Never."

"You've been a very patient girl," Paris said. "Do you think it will work out?"

"No. Not that way. Not now. Thank you for sending me out to the hospital."

"It was an errand of mercy."

"For whom?"

Paris grinned. "For Frank Montaigne, of course. Who else?"

Audrey Crystal smiled back. It seemed to Paris that she was more relaxed. The worried lines in her face had vanished. She looked happy and very much at ease.

"Of course," she said. "Who else?"

Paris stood for a moment. Then he reached into his pocket and pulled out his notebook. "One thing I came up to ask you. Did you ever hear of the word *Lowczyna?*"

"Low—what?"

"L-O-W-C-Z-Y-N-A. Lowczyna."

"No. I never heard of it. It sounds foreign. Polish?"

"Yes."

"I'm not familiar with it. What does it mean?"

"Female hunter. Huntress."

"Oh," she said. She looked up at him. "Was that Mrs. Huntress's real name?"

"Yes. Do you know of anybody connected in any way with the Institute who has that name or a name resembling it?"

"No." She smiled ruefully. "It's rather obvious now, isn't it? Somebody at the American Consulate in Bonn must have Anglicized her name to make it easier for her. Funny, I never gave it a thought. She never told that to Mrs. Copel, our interpreter."

"I know," Paris said. "We spoke to Mrs. Copel. We found out from her that Mrs. Huntress had a husband who got in trouble over another woman. He shot the woman's husband during a heated argument and then fled the country. That's the last she ever saw of him." Paris slipped the notebook back into his pocket. "When will Doctor Raeder be back?"

"At four this afternoon."

"I wonder if you'd ask him to be kind enough to drop around to my office when he returns from his meeting."

"I'll tell him."

"Thank you." He reached into his jacket pocket and pulled out a card. "This will tell him where to find me." He dropped the card on her desk.

The telephone by her elbow rang. She answered it. "It's for you, Captain."

He picked up the receiver and said, "Paris." He listened for a moment and then said, "Right away." He hung up and motioned to McKenney. Then he said, "Good-by, Mrs. Crystal."

180

They went out of the room and down the stairs. McKenney asked, "What's up?"

"Summerton again," Paris said.

They went racing into Summerton, McKenney driving the Mercury. They turned in at Avalon Street. The street was crowded with people. They were being moved back to the opposite sidewalk by two Summerton policemen and a state trooper. McKenney pushed the car through, their siren churning. The people gave way slowly until they were able to pull up in front of the house. The trooper came over and peered in. Then he opened the door.

Paris jumped out and went into the narrow building. McKenney followed him in. They ran up the stairs to the second floor. Chief of Police Matt Hruska was there in the dimly lit hallway, flattened against the wall. On the other side of him was Detective-Lieutenant Walter Franz of the State Police. Each had his revolver out.

Hruska said, "It's Ducky Britt. He's in there. He's got a gun and won't come out. Threatened to kill one of us and then turn the gun on himself."

Paris looked at Franz, who was pressed back against the banister of the staircase leading to the floor above. "I was tailing him, Captain," he said. "He came up here to Maddox's apartment. He must have had a key. I followed him up and listened at the door. I heard him chopping away at something. I tried the door and it was locked. He called out that he had a gun and he'd shoot if we didn't go away."

Paris glanced at Hruska. "Ducky is a little soft in the squash, Wade," he said. "He just might do that."

181

"Did you see a gun on him?" Paris asked Franz.

"No, sir," Franz said.

"Who's covering the back?"

Hruska said, "Moriarty and one of my boys, Sam Basilia."

"How about the roof, Matt?"

"Two floors above here," Hruska said. "We could lower a guy down to the window but he'd be a sitting duck as a target."

"Well, now," Paris said. "Ducky only *said* he has a gun. Did anybody see it?"

Hruska said, "Sam Basilia came around the back and Ducky waved a gun at him. Told him to get back or he'd shoot."

"Do you mind?" Paris asked Hruska.

Hruska smiled. "Go ahead, Wade. This one is on me."

Paris called, "Britt! Put down your gun, open the door and come out with your hands up. You haven't got a chance."

"Keep away," a sobbing, hysterical voice called back. "I'll kill all of you."

Paris stepped back, reached under his coat and took out his snub-barreled revolver. He raised his right leg and kicked the door hard with his heel. The door creaked and sagged but held. He kicked again. The door flew open. Inside the room, Britt was facing him, a gun in his fist.

"Drop it," Paris said sharply.

The man dropped his gun. Paris went in swiftly and grabbed him. Franz was beside him, twisting the man around and putting the handcuffs on his wrists behind his back. Hruska reached under Britt's arms and began searching through his coat. He reached into a side pocket and brought out a sheaf of money. He flipped it with his thumb.

Paris bent down and picked up the gun. It was a black plastic pistol. The words "Texas Ranger" were printed in white lettering across the handle.

"Damn fool," Paris said. "You could have got yourself killed."

"Now what did you cause all that trouble for?" Hruska said.

"That money's mine," Britt said. His lips quivered. He blinked twice and squinted up at him. "That money's *mine.*"

The room was warm and the air was damp and heavy. The only thing that looked out of order was the hearth in front of the fireplace. The brass andirons had been pulled away and were lying to one side. There was a pile of blackened bricks stacked beside them. It looked as if they had been chipped away from the back of the fireplace. He went over, knelt down and peered inside. The back brick wall had been taken down, the mortar chipped away with a hammer and chisel which lay on the floor near Paris' feet. Paris picked up the chisel and pried one of the loose bricks away. The brick fell down. Taped against the back were some bills. He peeled them off. There were five one-hundred-dollar bills.

He walked back to Britt. "Well?" he asked.

"It's mine, Captain. He left it to me. He had about thirty thousand bucks behind those bricks. I was the one who helped him cement the dough in there."

"What was it for?" Paris asked.

"Fall money," Britt said. "In case he got into trouble. He don't need it now. He said to me then, Ducky, if anything ever happens to me, the dough's yours."

"If you can prove it," Hruska said.

"Sure, I can prove it. I bought the cement. Ask Miller down at the hardware store."

"We'll need a little more proof than that. Who else knew about this money?"

"Nobody."

"The time Dewey was killed, somebody went through this place like a tornado. Who?"

"Beats me. Nobody would ever find it, but me. I know the cops tapped the whole place for hollow spots. But there weren't any. I know. I made the hideaway myself." He turned and moved slowly to the door. "I must have done something wrong," he said.

"You were too hungry, Ducky," Hruska said. "You just didn't wait long enough."

CHAPTER

24

WADE PARIS sat behind his office desk and finished reading through some State Department reports that had just come in. He looked up at the wall clock. It was ten minutes after four and he was tired. He swiveled slowly in his chair and propped his feet against the small radiator underneath the window. He folded his hands and waited. He heard footsteps along the corridor and then a knock on his door.

"Yes," he said.

A uniformed sergeant put his head in the doorway. "Captain, there's a Doctor Raeder to see you," he said.

"Thanks. Send him in."

He stood up and stretched. He heard another pair of footsteps approaching and then Dr. Raeder walked into the office. His hat was in his hand. He looked fresh and cool and immaculate. Paris came around the desk and shook hands with him.

"Thanks for coming, Doctor," he said. "Have a seat."

Raeder sat down. He placed his hat neatly in his lap.

Paris reached into his pocket and brought out a crumpled pack of cigarettes. He offered one, but Raeder shook his head.

"No, thank you, Captain," he said. "I prefer my own if you don't mind."

"Mrs. Crystal gave you my message?" Paris asked.

"That is why I am here," Raeder said. "I presume this is of great importance?"

"Oh, yes," Paris said. "I wouldn't take up your time or mine, otherwise." He walked over to the window and squinted through the Venetian blind. He stood for a moment and then said, "Now I'm not sure where this discussion will lead us, Doctor. So I must warn you that anything you say may be used as evidence."

Raeder's eyebrows arched. "Evidence of what?"

"We'll come to it," Paris said.

"The warning then seems like nonsense."

"A legal formality, Doctor," Paris said. "Quite British. But our common law in the Commonwealth of Massachusetts derives from the Anglo-Saxon, and we try to live up to the formalities."

"I understand all that," Raeder said.

"It differs from the French and German law in many ways. And the Polish, too." Paris walked behind his desk and sat down.

"I am aware of all this," Raeder said. "Will you please come to the point, Captain?"

"Of course." Paris leaned back in his chair and folded his arms. "Doctor Raeder, the Boston police have had you under surveillance for over a week."

186

Raeder pressed down on the brim of his hat. His forehead became ridged. "The police?" he said.

"Under close surveillance. They know, and we know, exactly what you've been doing all the time."

"Captain, if that is all the police have to do—"

"I'm sure you know what they found out. Lorraine Atwood?"

Raeder reached into his coat pocket and brought out his gold cigarette case. He opened it slowly and then very deliberately pulled out a cigarette. "If this is some devious attempt at blackmail, Captain," he said. He tapped the cigarette sharply against the case and then lit it with his lighter. "I know the police in this country are capable of doing despicable things. But my wife is not without influence—"

"Come, come, Doctor Raeder." Paris shifted down in his swivel chair and revolved it slightly toward the man. "Blackmail? How many men in Boston like you visit girls like Lorraine Atwood? Thousands. How many men friends does Miss Atwood have? Dozens? Hundreds? You'd be surprised at the number, Doctor Raeder. I've spoken to her, Doctor. An attractive girl. Twenty-seven. Nice figure. This year her hair is blonde. She has nice manners. She's well behaved and she's very discreet. Her apartment is in a large building. It makes it hard to find out the number of her visitors. On her income-tax form she lists herself as an entertainer. Who can say that isn't a perfect title for her? But between what she reports and what she earns—" Paris smiled and spread his hands—"I'm afraid the Department of Internal Revenue has that headache."

"I know no person by the name of Lorraine Atwood."

"Sure. You don't think I'd throw the girl's name at you and then expect you to break down and confess to adultery. You can deny it all you want. It doesn't matter. We have the evidence."

Raeder stood up quickly. "I will not sit here and be insulted—"

"No, no, sit down," Paris said. "We're not concerned with Miss Atwood. But we are concerned with a pattern. We've been looking for a pattern in this case and we've found it. And we've found it in Miss Atwood. Remember, I'm just a policeman, Doctor Raeder. You're the trained psychologist."

"I am afraid you have some weird ideas on psychology yourself, Captain."

Paris sat forward in his chair and then got to his feet. He walked over to the window and put one foot up on the radiator. "We're in the same business, Doctor," he said. "We both look for motivations. Our criminals are listed under what we call an M.O. file. *Modus operandi*. Method of operation. We know that each human mind has certain behavior traits." He stopped for a moment and then stepped back behind his desk. "Am I boring you, Doctor?"

"No. I'm beginning to become amused."

"Good, we'll both have a laugh over it. But you and I know that if you make up a certain set of circumstances and condition the person to them he will follow a certain pattern."

"You're referring to the experiments originally performed by the Russian psychologist, Pavlov."

"Yes," Paris said. "Ivan Petrovich Pavlov. He was the pioneer in the study of conditioned reflexes. He won the Nobel Prize in 1904 for his work."

"I'm quite familiar with Pavlov's work on dogs."

"Good. I was very much interested in his study of the digestive glands. Bring the ordinary person into a pitch-dark room and suddenly shout *boo* at him and his scalp will prickle and he'll sustain some shock. If he's hungry and you show him savory food, his mouth waters. Tell him an amusing story and he laughs. Put him in a cold room and he shivers. All very basic."

"Very elementary," Raeder said. He leaned forward and crushed his cigarette in the desk ash tray. Then he leaned back in his chair and said wryly, "Your interest in elementary psychology is quite heartwarming."

"Thank you," Paris said. "It's just all part of the job. Now let's carry it a step further. By *we,* I mean the police, because things are so common with us. We can take a man who marries a wealthy woman and we know that he too follows a pattern. Either he marries her for love or he marries her for her money. If it is sincerely for love, the man will follow one pattern. If he marries her for her money, he follows another pattern."

"If you think you're going to insult me again, Captain—"

"I'm not insulting you, Doctor. I'm talking straight facts. If you had met Mrs. Raeder in California, and it was a straight love match, I'd say fine, and good luck to both of you. You are a handsome man, Doctor Raeder. You carry yourself well. You have what a lot of us lack here—a certain courtliness of manner."

189

"Your efforts are crude, Captain," Raeder said. "And your flattery is transparent."

"I'm not flattering you, Doctor. I'm talking facts." Paris pulled gently at his lower lip and then leaned back in the chair. "Now a man either marries for love or for opportunity. The ones who marry for opportunity I call opportunists. Being opportunists, they are clever. They have to be. They got where they are by cleverness."

"Really, Captain. You're not talking to a school child."

"I know that," Paris said. "But first we've got to understand each other. Now the opportunist who marries for money first has to convince his marriage partner of his love and sincerity. The police know that. We couldn't function otherwise. I once knew of a very wealthy couple. The husband was very good-looking, the wife was ugly. My first impression was that the man had married his wife for her money. I was wrong. He was the rich one and he was very much in love with his wife. Why? Because she had tremendous charm and personality, a warmth and inner beauty. As soon as she spoke you forgot her physical unattractiveness. So I know these things are possible."

"What is this leading to, Captain?"

"Just this. You're a man of physical attractiveness, and you draw the admiration of women. If a man is in love with his wife he ignores these attentions. Sometimes he is oblivious to them. Sometimes he knows but it just doesn't reach him. You have a very pretty assistant in Mrs. Crystal. She's had an infatuation for you."

Raeder sighed and twisted in his chair. "I never had anything to do with Mrs. Crystal. I have ignored any manifestations."

"Exactly. That's where you misled us for a short time. But then, of course, an animal usually doesn't soil his own den, especially not an opportunist. It's much simpler to have someone like Lorraine Atwood. And there was the clue to the pattern we were looking for."

"What did you find out, Captain? That occasionally I visit another woman?"

"That's inconsequential. The important thing was for us to find out just what sort of man you are. We did. You are an opportunist, Doctor. Your marriage was for money and was carefully planned. Your position here at the Institute—"

"You will find that I am more than capable for the job."

"Yes. But you're living in luxury far beyond the salary for your type of job."

"Frankly, Captain, this discussion about my personal motivations is not only ridiculous but quite boring. Now if you don't have anything else—"

"Oh, there's something else, Doctor." Paris leaned over the desk and sorted through the loose pile of papers. He found one, held it in his hand for a moment and then dropped it back on the desk. He pursed his lips and said, "I have a report from the State Department. It's a short report, Doctor. But it's a very interesting one. It's interesting because behind all the official words and phrasing it tells a very intriguing story."

"I am afraid I do not know what you are talking about."

"I'm talking about the story of three men who had decided to flee from East Germany into West Germany a little over thirteen years ago. Two Germans and a Pole.

Their names were Fritz Raeder, Joseph Vomrath and Stanley Lowczyna. Do you know of this report?"

"I have some knowledge of it."

"*Some* knowledge? The report is in your own words."

"I know of it."

"According to your statement, the three men decided to cross the border by swimming the Elbe River near Dömitz. In the process of starting across they were fired on by Communist border guards. Two of the men were killed. The other survived. And that one survivor was you."

"Yes," Raeder said. "They shot us down. It was just along the bank of the river. I pretended to be dead. Then when they went off to get a wagon for our bodies, I slipped into the water and swam across the Elbe into the British zone near Dannenberg. Everybody knows that. It's all part of the record."

"Yes," Paris said. He looked up at the ceiling and smiled wryly. "Sometime ago I asked you if it wasn't odd that the name of the Polish refugee would be Marie Huntress. It was Anglicized. You saw nothing unusual about it." Paris paused and looked down at the desk. Then he sat up, propped his elbows on the green blotter. "Were you aware that the Polish word for *huntress* is *lowczyna?*"

"No."

"You speak Polish very well."

"I am not familiar with *all* the words."

"You had a man named Stanley Lowczyna in your party."

"I did not connect them."

"You can see what I'm driving at, can't you, Doctor?" Paris asked.

Raeder shrugged his shoulders and smiled. "I am afraid I cannot, Captain," he said.

"Well, then," Paris said, "let me spell it out for you. I suggest that you are Stanley Lowczyna. I suggest that the two men who died in the attempted escape were the two Germans, Joseph Vomrath and Fritz Raeder. You were the survivor. The Pole. Stanley Lowczyna."

"I am Doctor Fritz Raeder."

"No," Paris said. "We've identified you as Stanley Lowczyna, the husband of Marie Lowczyna."

"This is ridiculous," Raeder said. "I am not going to sit here and trade words back and forth with you, Captain—"

Paris interrupted him sharply. "We claim you assumed Raeder's identity when you reached the British zone. His family were all dead and he fitted your background and education the closest."

"Utter nonsense," Raeder said. "I would have no valid reason to assume any identity other than my own. If, as you say, I was a Pole, I would have had a much easier time entering America under the Polish quota. A German had more difficulty."

"Except that you were in trouble in Poland. You had shot a man. And it was not hard to establish yourself in West Germany as Fritz Raeder. Your German was as good as your Polish. True, you had a North European accent, but you knew Raeder had come from the Baltic area. You taught languages and psychology at the high school in Susz. Then later at Bremen, Germany. You came over on an exchange scholarship and once you were here you could become an American citizen. Must I go into more detail?"

193

"Everything you said is a lie. I am Fritz Raeder."

"To whom? You weren't to your wife, Marie Lowczyna. Somehow she found out you were in the Boston area. She came here to find you. That was bad. Marie was out of your life. You were now married to a rich American woman. You were a bigamist. All this would make your marriage to Cecelia Boyd invalid and you would be deported back to Communist Poland. Marie could cause all this. You met her for the first time at the dance of the Polish Cultural Society. First you gave her money and told her to be patient. But that did not solve the problem of two wives. You knew you had to have her killed."

"Whoever killed her, tried to kill me too," Raeder said. His lips were tight. The muscles of his jaw were knotted and his voice was harsh. "You know that an attempt was made on my life too."

"Oh, yes. The shot from the balcony." Paris managed a wry smile. He picked a pencil from the green blotter and tapped it softly against the edge of his desk. "The cleverness," he said. "Always the cleverness and the gimmick. All you did was complicate things and attract more attention to yourself. The clever criminals can never learn that. And it wasn't so fiendishly clever. A piece of thin, black twine tied to the electric fan and then brought loosely to the balcony outside your office. You tied a gun to the railing and aimed the muzzle high. The twine was tied to the trigger and looped around the butt. All you had to do was turn on the fan and go back to your desk. The fan spins drawing in the twine around the shaft, pulling the twine tighter, until it squeezes the trigger. The shot comes from the balcony over your head. Audrey Crystal is a good witness. You send her down to call for help. Why couldn't she use the telephone in the room? You had to get her out of the room. You had to dispose of the twine and put the gun on the fire ladder. Very clever."

"Ridiculous," Raeder said. He cleared his throat dryly. "You could never prove such a monstrous accusation."

"You were in Summerton. You met Dewey Maddox. You spoke to him, jokingly at first, about killing someone. Then it took on a serious vein. He said he could get someone to kill the person for you. We don't know what you offered Maddox as his share. But we do know that all you told Maddox was the person you wanted out of the way was at the Summerton Hospital. You went with Maddox to meet the hired killer on the road near Lake Islington. You wore a black stocking as a disguise and you hid in the car. The hired killer and Maddox began to talk. You became suspicious of the hired killer's questions, and when Maddox blurted out that the woman was at the Summerton Hospital, you panicked. Then you shot the stranger. You got into the car with Maddox and sped off. Maddox and you argued all the way to his office about the shooting. When you came into Summerton you went directly with Maddox to his office and decided to kill him for you were afraid he would shoot off his mouth. Then you turned the place upside down, looking for any evidence that might have linked you to Maddox. When you found none you had to complete the final step. You had to kill your wife Marie that very night."

"She was not my wife."

"You went up to her room and talked to her. You couldn't get anywhere with her so you struck her on the head and knocked her out. Then the cleverness again. You stuffed the windows and door cracks with newspapers. At the front door you had to attach the papers around the edges with cellophane tape because that was your only way out. Then you turned on the gas jets, went out and slammed the door. It locked automatically. That was it. You thought you had taken care of everything. Except that the so-called killer didn't die."

"Captain," Raeder said, "you have made grave accusations against me. I cannot allow you to continue with this fantastic story. I cannot allow you to talk to me in that fashion. I am a citizen of the United States."

"I don't think you are. Stanley Lowczyna is not a citizen of this country."

Raeder bowed his head. "I am speaking to you as Doctor Fritz Raeder. Because I am Doctor Fritz Raeder, and a citizen of this country. But even an alien is presumed innocent unless proven guilty. This is also in your Anglo-Saxon law. I have no statement to make. If you have nothing more to say to me as Doctor Raeder then I must go. You have your choice to either arrest me or release me, Captain."

Paris swung his chair around and stood up. He walked around his desk and sat down on the side edge. He crossed his feet and looked at Raeder. "Well, there is one thing more. We have a machine here which is a great help in our work. It's called a polygraph."

"A lie-detector machine?"

"Yes. You're familiar with it?"

"I am."

"We use it often."

"It is of no value as evidence," Raeder said.

"It's a very valuable means of getting evidence," Paris said. "But, as you say, it's not permissible in court."

"Then I can't see that it has any value."

"It helps us eliminate suspects who are innocent. There are any number of times when we have a suspect and we test him on the machine. If the test is in his favor we let him go."

"The machine can only be used voluntarily," Raeder said.

"That's right. It wouldn't work well any other way. The suspect must be willing to take the test. If he's innocent he's anxious to take it. He knows it will help to clear him."

Raeder smiled mirthlessly. "I understand."

"Then are you willing?"

"To take the lie-detector test?" asked Raeder.

"Yes."

"Why should I?"

Paris spread his hands. "Why not?" He walked to the window and tugged at the Venetian blind cord. The wooden slats clattered to the top of the window and the late afternoon sunlight spilled into the office. He looked down at the traffic below and said, "If you're not the person we want then that's the end of it. I'll apologize for the inconvenience and you won't be bothered again."

"This is ridiculous."

Paris turned. "I'm afraid it isn't," he said. "And I think you'll find verbal interrogation much harder."

"I'm an educated man, Captain. A trained psychologist. I know just how this machine works."

"That's all right," Paris said.

"This is a machine for the lower level mentality—the emotional type. It would be of no value to you, Captain. I know how to beat it."

"I'm willing to take the chance," Paris said. He moved back to the desk and sat down. "Now I say you're Stanley Lowczyna and you deny it. Don't you want to clear it up one way or the other?"

Raeder moved his shoulders. "It is merely that I consider it a waste of time."

"It won't take more than twenty minutes."

"You're a very deceptive man, Captain."

"Am I?"

"Yes. I had quite a different picture of the American police."

"What picture?"

"Bumbling, ignorant, naïve. Perhaps I have underestimated them."

"Why not find out?"

"You mean the machine? If I refuse you will consider it an admission of guilt?"

Paris shrugged his shoulders. "What would you think in my position? The machine won't lie."

"I am at your service, Captain," Raeder said.

CHAPTER

25

THE lie-detector office was on the fourth floor. It consisted
of two rooms, the larger of which was the testing room.
It was Spartanly furnished with two, straight-backed,
wooden chairs and a heavy desk which supported the thin,
black polygraph machine. The room was carefully sound-
proofed which made it unnaturally quiet. There was a
faint, stuffy odor in the air for all the windows had been
taped shut and the blinds pulled tight over the glass—
every precaution had been taken to obscure any outside
noises which might cause a distraction during the examination.

The second room was very small. Although it was not
connected to the testing room by a door, there was a sheet
of one-way glass installed in the wall so that investiga-
tors could watch unobserved as the test progressed. There
was a tape recorder on a small table near the window.
The cord which dropped down to the floor from its side
ran out through a hole in the baseboard to a small micro-

phone concealed in the mouthpiece of the dummy telephone on the testing room desk.

Wade Paris walked into the testing room with Raeder
and introduced him to Pat Muldowney. He did not give
Muldowney's rank as a detective-lieutenant. People taking
lie-detector tests were usually more comfortable when
they thought they were in the presence of a civilian employee. Muldowney was a medium-sized man with white
hair, a waved forelock of which slanted down across his
left eye. His blue cord suit was rumpled and there was a
thin line of perspiration over his upper lip.

"You can take over from here, Pat," Paris said. "I'll wait
outside until you're finished."

Muldowney nodded and Paris closed the door quietly behind him.

"You are a full-time employee of the State Police?"

"Yes, sir," Muldowney said. He had a soft, gentle, almost
apologetic voice. He was a man who had an intense interest in his work and a good, practical understanding of
human nature. He had the ability to get along with people
and to be well liked. He was the kind of man whom people
could feel comfortable talking with.

"What kind of machine do you have?" Raeder said.

"A Keeler Polygraph. A new one. The latest model. Do
you know of these things?"

"Yes. I am a psychologist."

"Good," Muldowney said. "It's going to make things easier."

"You do this all the time?"

"No, sir. I have other duties. Would you like to begin?"

Raeder nodded. "May I take off my coat?"

"You'll find a hanger over there," Muldowney said.

Raeder took off his coat, hung it up and sat down in the chair which was pushed up at right angles against the desk.

Muldowney said, "Make yourself as comfortable as you can. Loosen your tie if you wish."

"I am quite comfortable," Raeder said.

"As you know," Muldowney said, "there are three main parts to the polygraph. A galvanic skin electrode which measures perspiration. Then there's a blood-pressure cuff and a respiration tube to measure your breathing."

"I know of these things. Do you get good results?"

"Why, yes. About 10 per cent will confess as soon as they see the machine."

"Without the use of it?"

"Yes, sir."

"And the others?"

"It is over 90 per cent accurate."

"Do the guilty ones confess afterward?"

"Yes. Most of them do."

"Have you ever thought why, Mr. Muldowney?"

Muldowney smiled apologetically. "I'm not much up on those things, Doctor. I think there's a compulsion in people to confess their crimes. Human beings have a built-in conscience. Most of the time they can hardly wait to tell us everything. What is your opinion, Doctor?"

"They're fools," Raeder said. "Masochists. They have a desire to inflict punishment on themselves."

"Well," Muldowney said, "whatever it is, the compulsion is there."

"The machine is never completely correct, of course."

"Nothing in life is 100 per cent," Muldowney said. "Nothing except death—and that's not life. Oh, I find exceptions to the rules. That's what makes the work interesting."

"To be sure," Raeder said. "Do you wish me to roll up my sleeve?"

"No, it won't be necessary," Muldowney said. He fastened the rubber blood-pressure cuff around the upper part of Raeder's right arm. "Is that too tight?" he asked.

"No, quite comfortable, thank you." Raeder turned and looked up at Muldowney. "Have you studied the polygraph extensively?" he asked.

"Yes. In Chicago. And I've gone back for refresher courses. All in all I've handled the machine here for ten years."

"And the results have been accurate?"

"Oh, yes."

"If you have a normal patient."

"We don't test psychotics."

"Neurotics?"

"We're all more or less neurotic, Doctor. We live in a high-pressure civilization. Small neuroses are quite common. Sometimes they're even quite necessary." He smiled. "Now, sir, if you'll let me put the pneumograph tube over your stomach."

"Don't they usually put these across the chest?" Raeder said.

"Yes, some do," said Muldowney. "I prefer the stomach."

"It's comfortable," Raeder said, looking down at the black, corrugated rubber tube. "This is for the respiration?"

"Yes, sir. The breathing." He turned and walked behind the desk. "When I start the machine I'm going to ask you ten questions. If you murdered Marie Huntress, it will show up on the machine. If you murdered Dewey Maddox it will show up on the machine. If you shot the trooper Frank Montaigne it will also show up on the machine. If you are telling the truth the machine will show it. If you're not, the machine will show that, too. I hope I've made myself clear, Doctor."

"Perfectly," Raeder said. "I regret I will disappoint you."

Muldowney smiled. He sat down behind the desk and straightened the slim metal styluses against the sheet of lined graph paper. "There will be a wait between each question so that you can prepare yourself for the next one."

Raeder smiled scornfully. "That is to give the pens on the machine a chance to record their movements."

Muldowney sat forward in his chair and glanced down at his wrist watch. "Are you ready to begin?"

Raeder nodded impatiently. "Let us make it as quickly as possible. The time is getting late."

Muldowney nodded absently and took a pencil from his coat pocket. "Now I'm going to give you a general idea of what the test questions will consist of," he said.

Raeder looked surprised. "Really?" he asked.

Muldowney smiled. "We want to make certain that your thoughts will be concentrated on the subject at hand."

"I see," Raeder said.

Muldowney reached down and pulled a sheet of paper out of the desk drawer. "First, I'll ask you about Marie

Huntress," he said. "I'll ask you if you were ever in her room. I'll also ask you if you killed her. I'll ask you if you killed Dewey Maddox. Is that clear?"

"Of course."

Muldowney started the machine and the graph paper began to move slowly under the spidery tracings of the sharp stylus points. He had decided to give Raeder a controlled set of questions. Every other question would be connected with the crimes. If Raeder was lying, each denial would show an abrupt change in his respirational level and a rise in his blood pressure and pulse rate. "I want you to sit still, look straight ahead and answer all questions by just 'yes' or 'no,'" Muldowney said. "Is that clear?"

"Yes."

Muldowney glanced down at the long, slender second hand on his wrist watch as it swept across the face of the dial. "One— Are you taking this lie-detector test voluntarily?" he asked.

"Yes," Raeder answered.

The three pens wiggled, leaving three thin, wavy tracks across the moving paper. Muldowney made a plus sign underneath with his pencil. Then he shut off the machine. "Doctor Raeder," he said. "You took a quick, abnormal breath after I asked the question."

"I am sorry," Raeder said. "It was an involuntary reflex."

"Let's start again," Muldowney said. He pushed the switch and the graph paper began moving through the machine again.

"One— Are you taking this lie-detector test voluntarily?"

"Yes."

Muldowney marked the paper with a plus sign. Then he waited for ten seconds.

"Two— Did you kill Marie Huntress?"

"No."

Muldowney marked the graph paper with a minus sign. He waited for fifteen seconds.

"Three— Do you live in Boston?"

"Yes."

Muldowney marked a plus on the graph. He waited twenty seconds.

"Four— Were you ever in Marie Huntress's room?"

"No."

Muldowney drew a minus sign on the paper. He looked down at the second hand of his watch. The room was still and made the small movements of the polygraph machine abnormally loud.

"Five— Do you smoke?"

"Yes."

Muldowney crossed a plus sign. The sound of Raeder's breathing was faint and he glanced up slowly to see if he was holding it back. But Raeder's chest was rising and falling slowly. And the base level of his respiration, Muldowney could see, was showing a regular pattern on the moving paper.

"Six— Do you know who shot Dewey Maddox?"

"No."

The silence of the room was overpowering, and as Muldowney marked a minus sign, he wondered if the small scratch of his pencil lead against the graph paper was as loud to Raeder as it seemed to him.

"Seven— Are you now married to the former Cecelia Boyd?"

"Yes."

Muldowney penciled in a plus sign and waited twenty seconds.

"Eight— Does the name of Stanley Lowczyna have any particular meaning to you?"

"No."

Muldowney paused for a moment before marking a minus sign. He watched the styluses carefully. That had been the control question—the question to which he knew the correct answer. But Raeder couldn't know he was aware of the name Lowczyna and how it fitted in with the case. Had he noticed Raeder pausing for a moment before he had answered? Had Raeder, in that split second, tried to outguess him? Muldowney looked down at his watch.

"Nine— Were you born in Germany?"

"Yes."

Muldowney waited. He penciled in a plus sign and watched the paper move across the desk. It had reached the edge and was beginning to spill down over the side.

"Ten— Is your real name Stanley Lowczyna?"

Raeder started. Then, slowly, "No," he said. And then, "No, my name is *not* Stanley Lowczyna!"

Muldowney switched off the machine. "Just a minute, Doctor—"

"No, *not* just a minute!" He reached up and tugged at the rubber blood-pressure cuff. "I am tired and I am weary. I have been questioned and antagonized by Captain Paris and I have been questioned by you. I am tired of questions. As a matter of fact, I am *very* tired of questions."

Muldowney came quickly around the desk. He unfastened the rubber arm cuff and pulled the corrugated respiratory tube away from Raeder's stomach. "Why don't you stand up for a minute, Doctor?" he said. "Stretch your legs. I know that sitting in one position can become very tiring."

"Yes," Raeder said. "Very tiring. And the questions— the clever questions, they're very tiring, too." He stood up and took a few steps across the room. "Very, very tiring indeed."

Muldowney said, "It didn't take very long, did it?"

"A devilish nuisance," Raeder said. He rubbed his arm and walked over to the wall and took his coat off the hanger. "That will be all, won't it?"

"We didn't finish the examination," Muldowney said. "There was a card test. But I don't think we need to do that."

"No, I don't think so either," snapped Raeder. "I've had just about enough for today."

Muldowney walked to the door. "Excuse me for a moment, Doctor."

He went out. Raeder wandered around the room. He bent over the lie-detector machine and looked at the three pens and the various knobs and dials underneath them. He took out a cigarette and lit it slowly.

He heard footsteps in the hallway outside. Then the door to the room opened and Wade Paris came in. Behind him was Muldowney, holding the graph paper in his hand.

"How do you do, Captain," Raeder said.

"Well," Paris said. "Can we have a statement from you now?"

"On what?"

"Oh, come on," Paris said impatiently. "You know what. You lied."

"Where? Perhaps I showed some reaction to the last question. I was very tired and irritable."

Paris turned and took the graph paper from Muldowney. "Yes," he said. "You showed a reaction there. You also lied on questions two, four, six and eight."

"I was very nervous," Raeder said. He walked to the chair in front of the lie-detector machine and sat down. "I must see the graph for myself."

"You can read the polygraph, can't you?"

"Yes," Raeder said.

Paris slid the paper onto the table. "Here, you can see for yourself. There are the numbers of the questions. There are the plus and minus signs meaning you answered the questions either yes or no. You can see for yourself how the pens jumped."

"Yes, I see," Raeder said. He looked around thoughtfully.

"I'm sure that Fritz Raeder's fingerprints are on file somewhere in Germany. As an officer in the Wehrmacht he would have had them taken sometime during his career. We can check through. It might take a little time. But you can be sure we'll do it, one way or the other."

"Yes," Raeder said quietly. He inhaled slowly on his cigarette.

"Are you ready to make a statement?" Paris asked.

"I must think," Raeder said. "I must collect myself. If I could go out for a moment so that I could be alone with my thoughts."

"You can sit here for a while."

"I need some air."

"All right," Paris said. "Go out. Get some fresh air. Take a walk around the block. Then come back to my office and talk to me."

"Thank you, Captain," Raeder said. He looked at Muldowney. "Thank you. You were very competent."

Raeder put on his hat and adjusted it carefully. Then he went out of the room. He did not wait for the elevator but took the stairway instead.

When he came to the Babcock Street entrance he stopped for a moment to get his bearings. Then he turned right and walked briskly to the corner of Commonwealth Avenue. He stopped suddenly to look behind him and several pedestrians, their heads down, intent on going home, almost collided with him. Raeder saw that nobody had followed him from the building. He turned right and started toward the corner of Crowninshield Road. His car was parked at the curb halfway down the block. He took his car keys out and started to run. When he came to his car he quickly unlocked the door and slid behind the wheel. He put the key into the ignition.

A shadow moved out from behind the car parked in front and fell over him. The door was pulled open. He turned. A man said, "Get out."

He looked up at the man. He was tall and young. "Who are you?" he asked.

"Sergeant Styman, State Police," the man said. "Come on, Mister. Out."

"How dare you talk that way to me?" Raeder said.

"Out," Styman said.

"I'm not going with you," Raeder said hysterically.

"Come on, come on," Styman said.

Raeder gripped the wheel so tightly his knuckles whitened. He sat there rigidly, his feet planted tightly to the car floor. Styman reached in and put his right hand over Raeder's face, covering his nose and mouth and cutting off his breathing. With his other hand he grabbed Raeder's head and twisted it to the right. Raeder let go of the wheel and Styman pulled him out onto the pavement.

Raeder sat there, gasping for air. He saw another detective run up from the corner. The other man pulled him to his feet and locked Raeder's arm behind his back.

"Please," Raeder said. "Please, don't be cruel to me."

Styman looked at him sharply but made no reply.

CHAPTER

26

AUDREY CRYSTAL walked through the revolving glass doors into the Summerton Hospital. She carried a book wrapped in bright yellow paper in one hand and a small bouquet of flowers in the other. She spoke with the nurse at the reception desk and then went down the corridor, turned right and stopped before Trooper Frank Montaigne's room. The door was open. She knocked and looked inside. The room was empty. There was another door that led out to the screened veranda. She walked through the room and looked out.

He was sitting in a wicker chair staring out at the lawn. His arm was in a sling and he wore a maroon woolen robe. When he saw her he made an effort to get up.

"No," she said. "Please sit down." She pulled over a chair and sat down beside him. She noticed that his face was pale and boyish and noncommittal.

"You must have had so many visitors you've forgotten who I am."

"No, Mrs. Crystal," he said. "I know who you are."

"I went to visit Patty."

"Yes. My mother told me."

"She's an adorable child."

"Thank you."

She smiled and smoothed her skirt over her knees. "I've brought you something," she said. She held out the book and he put it on the table beside him.

"Thank you," he said.

"Do you think they'll let me put these flowers in a glass of water?"

"The glasses are free," he said. And then he smiled. "I think there's one on the sink inside."

She went into the room and in a moment she returned. "I've put them by your bed."

"Thank you."

"Look," she said. "I'm sorry about the questioning last time. But I had to find out. I was Raeder's assistant and I had to know."

"You mean Stanley Lowczyna."

"All right. Stanley Lowczyna. Have it your way."

"I had to know about the case," she said. "You see, I was in love with him."

"You were suspicious of him, weren't you?"

"No, not really. Just curious. He gave me nothing to be suspicious about. He was aloof from everybody. That's why it was so surprising to see him talking to Marie Huntress the night of the dance. It was just one of those things he never did. Then when she was murdered—"

"You began to worry."

"Yes," she said. She turned in her chair and looked out through the screen walls of the veranda. Some children were throwing a large red ball back and forth on the grass. They were laughing and calling to each other, and their high-pitched, excited voices carried back across to the lawn to where they sat. When she turned, Montaigne could see that her lips were quivering.

"Look, Mrs. Crystal—" he said.

"I admit I was infatuated with him. I admit it. Is that so terribly monstrous?"

"No," he said gently.

"You don't have to sit there so holy and everything—don't you know what it is to be lonely?"

"I know."

"I'm a divorcee. How do you feel about divorcees?"

"Everybody's entitled to a mistake."

"You don't think they're fair game?"

"No," he said. "Not you."

"Thank you. You see I had to tell you about Doctor—I mean, Stanley Lowczyna. I thought I was in love with him. That's as far as it went. There was no reciprocation."

"I know, Mrs. Crystal. He was too clever for that."

"Please," she said. "Audrey would be a lot nicer."

"How is Mrs. Raeder taking it?"

"She came in once. She hasn't been around the Institute since. She's very bitter and resentful."

"That's natural," he said.

"She's bitter about the police. Why?"

"Human nature," he said. "If the police hadn't found out about the murders she'd still have a husband."

"But he's a murderer."

213

"She wouldn't have known. She would have been happier that way."

"You're not serious, are you?" Audrey Crystal asked.

"Yes," he said. "Quite serious."

"But she's better off knowing what he was."

"Is she? It wrecked everything for her. No, I'm sorry but that's the way some people are."

She let her breath out slowly. "Yes, I guess I can understand." She turned her head and looked at him. "When are you leaving here?" she asked.

"Tomorrow. Look, Audrey, I started to ask you before—" He stopped and she noticed a flush beginning to spread across his cheeks. He opened his hands and grinned. "I'd like to come and see you sometime."

"I want you to," she said. "I hope you like spaghetti."

"Very much," he said.

"Good," she said. "I make it a special way. Would you bring Patty with you? I'd like to see her again."

He leaned back in the chair and smiled. "Of course," he said. "I think she'd like to see you again, too."

Dr. Valerian Zawisza sat in the den of his house reading the Boston paper. It was his favorite chair near the fireplace and his attention was pleasantly divided between the evening news and the excerpts from *Aida* which were being played over his stereophonic sound system. His wife was sitting opposite him, pulling at the long fingers of one hand with the other. She looked restlessly out of the picture window to the lights of the hospital below. Then she turned back to her husband.

"What does the paper say, Valerian?" she asked.

"About what?"

"About the case."

"Read it and you will find out."

"I have no patience to read," she said. "I want you to tell me."

"The murderer has confessed," he said.

"Why?" she asked. "They must have tortured him unspeakably."

"No," Zawisza said. "There was no way out. They knew everything. They had all the evidence."

"Were you surprised?"

"Yes, very much."

"Such impeccable judgment you have. You, a Pole. He fooled you completely."

"Yes. But first I am a Polish-American. I do not know all the nuances of the Polish language. Even in America a person from Vermont and one from Mississippi have far different speech patterns. In China there is such a far range of dialects that many people cannot even understand each other. I remember it was necessary at one time for them to converse in what they called Mandarin Chinese. A sort of national Esperanto."

"You make excuses for your ignorance so glibly."

"No," he said wearily. He opened his paper. "What difference does it make?"

"I knew he was not a German."

"How did you know?"

"I sensed it."

"You are more clever than I am," he said. "To me the

man's name was Fritz Raeder and he had a Northern German accent, or so it seemed."

"A very cultured man," she said. "He came here to the hospital. He was so efficient, so exacting, so well mannered. He was always so kind to me." She leaned back in her chair and ran her thin finger along the smooth edge of the end table. "What happened to the real Fritz Raeder? Did he kill him, too?"

"They are curious whether he did or not. It is not in their jurisdiction and it really isn't necessary. He has confessed to the murder of his wife and of Dewey Maddox. That is all they need."

"There is more to it than that, of course," she said, smiling. "You know it and I know it."

He put the paper down on his lap and stared at her quietly. "We know what, Gerda?"

"Oh, yes, we know, don't we?" she said. "He found out you were having an affair with his wife, Marie, and he had to kill her to save his honor."

He made no answer but lifted up the paper and studied it for a moment.

"You can't deny it because it's true," she said. "You can't hide those things from me. He was a man of great honor."

"Gerda," he said quietly. "You're sick. Why don't you go to bed?"

"Don't be afraid," she said. "I won't go to the police. The secret will die with me like all the other secrets I know about you."

"Yes," he said. "Let them die. There's no other way."

"But you must tell me one more thing," she said.

216

"Yes, Gerda?"

"Who is going to be your next sweetheart?"

"I haven't picked one yet," he said. "I will let you know when I do."

"No, you won't, but I will find out anyway. I have ways of finding out things, don't I?"

"Oh, yes," he said. "You have ways of finding things out to fit anything you want to believe."

"I'm a very ingenious woman, you know," she said lightly. "And very curious. And a very loyal wife too—"

She stopped and watched her husband get up from his chair. He crossed the room and adjusted a knob on the amplifier. She started to say something else, but the clear soprano's voice rose sharply in volume, filling the room with "Rittorna Vincitor," drowning out her half-started sentence with *Aida's* most famous aria.

Wesley Cagle was standing in the hot, steaming car washroom. He was in his undershirt and was wearing big rubber hip boots. A car moved slowly by him, linked to the chain system on the floor. He dipped the dripping mop into the detergent and lathered the lower portion of the car.

He heard his name being called. He twisted his head and looked up. From the open office window he saw his brother-in-law, Al Weaver. Al had his fawn-colored Stetson on and there was a big cigar in his mouth.

"What the hell's the matter with you?" Al shouted. "You're slow. Keep moving. Keep moving, dammit."

Cagle dipped the mop again hurriedly, cursing Al Weaver under his breath. It was a busy day and Weaver had sped up the chain system to push the cars through faster. His arms were leaden and heavy and they ached. He had trouble breathing in the hot, steamy air. He knew the other men were not working as hard. They knew when to coast, and many of the cars came off the line only superficially washed and partly dried. Across from him, his partner Tony Berry seemed to be working industriously. But Tony was faking too. He had the advantage of facing the office and he could see whether Al Weaver or the foreman was watching.

Tony Berry needed money too. He was a slow, phlegmatic person who had a record of petty thievery. They had talked several times at their half-hour lunch period. Tony Berry had said the best thing to hold up was a gas station. There'd been a lot of them lately and nobody had been caught.

"I got caught last time," he had said to Tony.

"Yeah," Tony said. "Well, you gotta be more careful, I guess. These other guys are getting away with it."

"I don't have a gun any more," he had said to Tony.

"I got one," Tony said.

"It can be done," Wes Cagle had told him. Gas stations always had money. You had to case them first and figure the best time for the job. You had to go in and out. You had to make it quick.

Tony Berry had agreed with him and now as he dipped the mop into the soap he knew he was going to ask Berry to go out with him. He just couldn't take it any more at the car-wash place. He had tried his best. He really had. Tomorrow night he'd ask Berry. Not tonight. Tonight the parole officer was coming.

Ruth Cagle moved the groceries past her at the super-market checkout counter. She pushed them past with one hand and punched the keys of the cash register with the nimble fingers of the other. She was doing it automatically, only half seeing the objects and the blue-stenciled prices as she pushed them by. There was a mechanical little smile on her face as a customer chatted with her. She did not listen. Her thoughts were on Wesley. Each night he came home in complete exhaustion, more morose and more sullen than the night before. She knew it could not last. One of these days he would quit and then—she didn't want to think of the next part.

She knew it was deliberate on Al Weaver's part. In some perverted way he was exacting some sense of satisfaction against her by getting at Wes. She had gone to Louise, and Louise had lost her temper and had accused her of whining and ingratitude and then plain jealousy. If it had not been for the kindness of her husband, she had said, Wes would still be in jail where he belonged. That had led to more words and then there had been a bigger flare-up and Louise had ordered her from the house, telling her that now she would see that Wesley got fired.

So, instead of making things better she had made them worse. She had not told Wesley anything and now she knew that she had nobody to go to and there was nothing more she could do. The inevitable was coming and she was completely helpless to do anything about it.

At the same time, at State Police Headquarters, there had been the regular monthly meeting of the troop commanders. The meeting was held in the Commissioner's office. Heading it were the Commissioner and Lieutenant Colonel Hines, who commanded the uniformed branch. Wade Paris sat in on the meeting in an advisory capacity. The main business was completed and now they were discussing the rash of gas-station stick-ups in the Dedham, Westwood, Norwood and Summerton areas. Captain Johanssen of Troop A said he could stop it and was asking for an increase of patrols in his area if somebody could spare more men. Colonel Hines said they would immediately siphon off men from Troops C and D and bring them in to cover every gas station in the area by patrolling in unmarked cruiser cars.

When the meeting was finished, Paris went back to his office and looked at the jumble of notes on his desk. There was a double suicide. A report of marijuana in a school area. A bank embezzlement. A reported bribery of a state official in northern Massachusetts. There was also a note that said *Cagle*. He decided he would do that first.

With the start given them by Cagle, they had broken the Maddox-Huntress case. Paris had spoken to some people about getting Cagle a better job. A machine shop in Hyde Park had promised Paris to give Cagle a job at the prevailing wage scale. This would be more than two and a half times what Cagle was earning now. Paris remembered that Cagle's parole officer was Joe Tallino. Tallino was a good man. He was quiet, dogged and very dedicated to his job.

Paris sat down in his chair, picked up the telephone and called him.

THE END

220

www.ingramcontent.com/pod-product-compliance
Lightning Source LLC
Chambersburg PA
CBHW031405250626
47155CB00004B/1425